The Basket Case

Volume 9 of

The Casebooks

Of Octavius Bear

Harry DeMaio

"Alternative Universe Mysteries for Adult Animal
Lovers"

Paperback 978-1-78705-349-6
ePub ISBN 978-1-78705-350-2
PDF ISBN 978-1-78705-351-9

Published in the UK by MX Publishing
335 Princess Park Manor, Royal Drive,
London, N11 3GX
www.mxpublishing.co.uk

Cover layout and construction by
Brian Belanger

Dedicated to GTP

A Most Extraordinary Bear

Acknowledgements

These books have evolved over a long period of time and under a wide range of influences and circumstances. I am indebted to many people for helping to bring Octavius and his cohorts to the printed page. Thanks most especially to my wife, Virginia, for her insights and clever suggestions as well as her unfailing enthusiasm for the project and patience with its author. To my sons, Mark and Andrew and their spouses, Cindy and Lorraine, for helping make these tomes more readable and audience friendly. To Cathy Hartnett, cheerleader-extraordinaire for her eagerness to see this alternate universe take form. To Jack Magan, Paul Bernish, Dan Andriacco, Amy Thomas, Luke Benjamin Kuhns and Zohreh Zand for their enthusiastic encouragement.

Kudos to Jim Effler, the late Bob Gibson and Brian Belanger for their wonderful illustrations and covers. Thanks, of course, to Steve Emecz and Timi at MX Publishing for giving Octavius et al. a great home

If, in spite of all this support, some errors or inconsistencies have crept through, the buck stops here. Needless to say, all of the characters, situations, and narratives are fictional. Many of the locations, vehicles and devices are not.

Also from Harry DeMaio

The Casebooks of Octavius Bear

1-The Open and Shut Case

2-The Case of the Spotted Band

3-The Case of Scotch

4-The Lower Case

5-The Curse of the Mummy's Case

6-The Attaché Case

7-The Suit Case

8-The Crank Case

9-The Basket Case

The Development of Civilization
Volume Nine - Part One
<u>Our Origins</u>

(From "An Introduction to Faunapology" by Octavius Bear Ph.D.)

About 100,000 years ago, according to scientific experts, a colossal solar flare blasted out from our Sun, creating gigantic magnetic storms here on Earth. These highly charged electrical tempests caused startling physical and psychological imbalances in the then population of our world. The complete nervous systems of some species were totally destroyed. For example, "Homo Sapiens" lost all mental and motor capabilities and rapidly became extinct. Less developed species exposed to the radiation were affected differently. Four-footed and finned mammals, birds and reptiles suddenly found themselves capable of complex thought, enhanced emotions, self-awareness, social consciousness and the ability to communicate, sometimes orally, sometimes telepathically, often both. Both speech production and speech perception slowly progressed with the evolution of tongues, lips, vocal cords and enhanced ear to brain connections. Many species developed opposable digits, fingers or claws, further accelerating civilized progress. Some others (most fish and underground dwellers) were shielded from the radiation and remained only as sentient as they were before the blast. This event is referred to as The Big Shock. It remains under intensive study.

The Players

- **Octavius Bear** – Mega-sized Kodiak; Narcoleptic war hero; Consulting Detective; Scientist; Inventor; Seeker of Justice; Gazillionaire owner of Universal Ursine Industries; Gourmet/Gourmand; Bee Keeper; Somewhat sedentary and grouchy just on general principles.

- **Mauritius (Maury) Meerkat** – Narrator; Assistant to Octavius; Theatrical Agent; African *émigré* with a French-Dutch background; clever with a shady history.

- **Bearoness Belinda Béarnaise Bruin Bear** *(nee Black)* – Gorgeous polar superstar, with the Aquashow, ***"Some Like It Cold;"*** Wife of Octavius; Extremely rich widow of Bearon Byron Bruin living in her castle/resort Polar Paradise in the Shetlands; Owner-pilot of the last flying Concorde SST.

- **Arabella Bear** – Hybrid bear cub prodigy; Twin daughter of Bearoness Belinda and Octavius.

- **McTavish Bear** – Hybrid bear cub prodigy; Twin son of Bearoness Belinda and Octavius.

- **Mlle Woof** – Bichon Frisé – Governess to the twin cubs.

- **Frau Schuylkill** – Octavius' beautiful Swiss she-wolf estate manager/cook/pilot/security officer with many other mysterious and military talents. She rescued Octavius from his dive off the Breakurbach Falls while he was struggling with his nemesis, Imperius Drake.

- **Wyatt Where** – Another wolf; Former military intelligence officer who had retired to a security post at the Bank of Lake Michigan in Chicago and then quit to join Octavius.

- **Howard Watt** – Porcupine; High tech security authority who also left the Bank to join Octavius; Alternate Universe specialist; Laser and particle beam accelerator expert.

- **Otto the Magnificent – aka Hairy Otter** – An absolutely terrible illusionist magician, Otto the Magnificent escaped the claws of super villain Imperius Drake but not before he developed some amazing powers courtesy of Imperius' genetic alterations.

- **Benedict and Galatea Tigris** – White Bengals; The Flying Tigers; Pilots of Belinda's and Octavius' aircraft; brother and sister.

- **Chita** – Beautiful, fascinating, clever, sexy, immoral and highly independent feline who among other things, is the publisher and editor-in-chief of *PURR* and *SOW* magazines.

- **L. Condor** – Andean Condor; cyber-net genius with a twelve-foot wingspan and artificial voice.

- **Marlin** – Dolphin (sic) the Prince of Whales' Chief Scientist, Magician and part time Jester.

- **Ernie Elks** – Head Coach of the Gotham Giraffes Basketball Team.

- **Joe Jeau Giraffe** – Star Power Forward for the Gotham Giraffes.

- **Ozzie Ostrich** – Center for the Omaha Hombres.

- **Omar Ostrich** – Center for the Orlando Orbiters.

- **Otis Ostrich** – Power Forward for the Orlando Orbiters.

- **Jerry Basen** – Basenji; Lawyer for the Gotham Giraffes.

- **Joni Cockatoo** – Defense Attorney for Joe Jeau Giraffe.

- **"Dunk" Duncan** – Red Kangaroo; Managing Director of the United Basketball Association.

- **Oscar Ostrich** – Coach of the Orlando Orbiters.

- **Osgood Ostrich** – Owner and head coach of the Omaha Hombres basketball team.
- **Osmond Ostrich** – Power Forward for the Omaha Hombres.
- **Olivia** – Ostrich Supermodel.
- **Wellington Weasel Esq.** – Olivia's lawyer.
- **Arlene Armadillo** – Olivia's agent.
- **Alfonso Aardvark** – Fashion Designer.
- **Greta** – Red Fox; Fashion Designer.
- **Farrah and Fergus Ferret** – TV Reporters
- **Rocky Raccoon** – Manager of the Rim Shot Sports Bar.
- **Captain Gordon Gorilla** – NYPD Detective.
- **Bill Bison** – Assistant Director of the FBI Criminal Investigative Division.
- **Malcolm Malamute** – FBI Special Agent – New York District.
- **Ursula 8** – Universal Ursine Intellect Model 8 – Artificial General Intelligence System.

Locations

Cincinnati, Ohio; UUI-Kentucky; New York City; and Alternate Universes

Octavius

Prologue

Do Bears give you a scare? Well, me too!

So, I'll pass on this tactic to you.

You just fix that old Bear

With a cold, piercing stare,

But make sure that he's Winnie-the-Pooh.

Hello and welcome to Octavius Bear's latest adventure – The Basket Case! My name is Maury *(Mauritius)* Meerkat - also known as Offscreen Narrator. When I am part of the action, I am Octavius' trusted associate and field captain. I am 2 feet tall plus tail and I weigh in at 24 pounds. Octavius, on the other hand, is a huge Kodiak – over 9 feet high and 1400 pounds – and like many of his species given to emotional outbursts.

As you may also know, among his many talents and accomplishments, he is a brilliant, self-taught practitioner in the wide-ranging fields of biology, physics, ursinology, psychology, voodoo, teleology, chemistry, apiculture and oenology. He is a self-made gazillionaire and sole owner of UUI *(Universal Ursine Industries.)* He is also a first rate electrical, electronic, structural, marine, computer science, aeronautical, civil, mechanical and chemical engineer. He has a few other interesting characteristics such as falling into brief, deep narcoleptic comas – side effects of his successful genetic experiments to eliminate the need for him to hibernate.

However, the talent and occupation that should interest you most is his avocation for criminology. The Bear works in close concert with Inspector

Bruce Wallaroo from Australia, of whom more later, and with his own Cincinnati based team:

- Frau Ilse Schuylkill – Swiss she-wolf; Bear's Lair estate manager; Cordon Bleu chef; jet pilot, detective and sharpshooter with other very strange and arcane abilities.

- Colonel Wyatt Where – another wolf; ex-military hero; security specialist and pilot; Frau Schuylkill's equally bizarre running mate.

- Doctor Howard Watt – porcupine; exceptional scientist and technologist; laser and weapons specialist; Quantum physics and Multiverse expert.

- Marlin – Brilliant dolphin; on loan from the Prince of Whales and Partner to Howard Watt

- Hairy Otter aka Otto the Magnificent - An absolutely terrible illusionist magician, Otto the Magnificent escaped the claws of super villain Imperius Drake but not before he developed some amazing powers courtesy of Imperius' genetic alterations.

- L. Condor – Andean Condor; cyber-net genius with a twelve-foot wingspan and artificial voice.

- Ursula – Universal Ursine Intellect Model 8 – Artificial General Intelligence System.

- Your humble servant – African Meerkat; Octavius' indispensable assistant; operative; scribe; overall facilitator; talent agent as well as a pretty clever detective, if I do say so myself.

When we are not out scouring the world for evildoers, in cooperation with local, national and international constabularies, we are headquartered in a rambling old mansion near Cincinnati which encompasses not only the Great

Bear's opulent digs, but his massive laboratories and shops; his missile silo *(don't ask!)* disguised as an Asian pagoda; and a large Roman temple that serves as a hangar for his four aircraft: a Twin Otter; a F15E Strike Eagle; a V-22 Osprey; a C5A-The Ursa Major; plus an AgustaWestland AW101 VVIP luxury helicopter -The Ursa Minor.

Currently on her supersonic way from Polar Paradise, her resort / castle in the Shetland Islands to the Bear's Lair in Cincinnati, Octavius' consort, Bearoness Belinda Béarnaise Bruin Bear (nee Black) is at the controls of the Aquabear, the last flying Concorde SST. She's joined by Benedict and Galatea Tigris, The Flying Tigers, who are acting as co-pilot and flight engineer. The Bearoness *(Bel to her friends and relations)* is a highly accomplished pilot of both fixed wing and rotary aircraft. Between her and Octavius, they own an impressive fleet of flying machines.

To retain her Bearonial status, Bel must occupy the castle at least six months of the year. She and Octavius do a supersonic commute between their opulent homes accompanied by their twin Cubs, Arabella and McTavish, and their governess, Mlle Woof. Much more of them, later.

The Great Bear had just received a call from Ernie Elks in New York City, his former classmate at Kodiak University. Ernie, once a formidable athlete himself, is the Head Coach of the Gotham Giraffes, a world-renowned pro basketball team. His star forward has just been arrested on suspicion of murder and Ernie wants to call in Octavius to investigate. He had once helped the Great Bear get Universal Ursine Industries off the ground with a substantial loan. Although Octavius had paid him back with sizeable interest, he still feels an obligation to Ernie, to say nothing of being an avid fan of the Giraffes. So, as soon as Belinda arrives with the Cubs and Mlle Woof, their governess, we are going to pack up and head for New York. That's fine with me. I have a passion for the Big Apple.

"What do you know about professional basketball, Maury?"

"Not much. I once played guard for the Kalahari Komets when I was in school. We were in the Pee-Wee Conference. Our ball had a six-inch circumference, the rim was four feet from the floor and the entire court was twenty feet long. I had a mean jump shot. We never got into the league finals, though. I have never seen a pro basketball game."

"Well, you're about to. Ernie Elks has been coaching the Super-Tall Gotham Giraffes for years and he has championship rings on all his antlers to show for it. The Super-Tall league includes giraffes, ostriches, camels, storks and emus. Tall but relatively slim."

"The Super-Large conference involves elephants, rhinos, hippos, large bears, elk, moose, some deer, horses and gorillas. They are more likely to play American football, rugby or other contact sports but there is a residual basketball league as well."

"Then, there is a vast number of small, medium and large leagues encompassing most of the other full and smaller-size mammals – lions, tigers, wolves, foxes, sheep, donkeys, even domestic cats and dogs. The Pee-Wee leagues are primarily school teams. Birds and amphibians have their own unique athletic events and organizations."

"So," I asked, "Is this star Giraffe forward accused of killing another giraffe?"

"No," the Bear replied, "It was an ostrich. That's all I know."

"Do Giraffes play against Ostriches?"

"Not that I know of. If they do, it's very seldom. Maybe in conference playoffs."

"Well, if nothing else, the Cubs will have a chance to see New York City."

"They'll probably want Belinda and me to buy it. They should be arriving shortly."

Chapter One

Polar Bears are a dazzling sight

With their wonderful coats of pure white.

But the skin on their back

Is a deep shade of black,

And their fur's just reflecting the light.

No sooner said…

Once again, its engines screaming and its "droop snoot" lowered to permit forward visibility, the Aquabear Concorde taxied smoothly up the runway, turned and stopped in front of the Bear's Lair near Cincinnati. Bearoness Belinda Béarnaise Bruin Bear (nee Black) was pilot in command assisted by Benedict and Galatea Tigris, The Flying Tigers, distinguished by their snow-white and black striped pelts.

Lolling in the rear near the galley, with a bowl of champagne in her paws was the incomparable Chita. Once a villainess of sorts, she has since become one of our crime-fighting partners. *(See Book Two -The Case of the Spotted Band)* As publisher/editor-in-chief of Purr and Sow magazines and their associated electronic media and TV sites, she was going to New York to take in Fashion Week. Bel had offered her a free ride and had stopped in London to pick her up.

Up front, in the narrow passenger compartment, the Cubs *(Arabella and McTavish)* were trying to get past Mlle Woof, their Bichon Frisé governess, and out the door.

"Attendez, mes petits. No one disembarks until the stairs are in place and the door is opened by the Flight Engineer. Back in your seats."

Polar Pouts! "It takes longer to get out of this plane than it does to fly here!"

"You will have plenty of additional flying time when we go to New York."

"Noo Yuck!" shouted McTavish, "We're going to Noo Yuck?"

"Oui! On the Ursa Minor."

"I love helicopters. When do we leave?"

"When your Momma and Poppa say so."

McTavish rushed up to the cockpit with Mlle Woof in pursuit. He pulled open the door and shouted, "Momma, when do we leave for Noo Yuck?"

"Shortly! Poppa, Maury, Frau Ilse, Colonel Where, Chita, Otto and Condo will be coming with us in the Ursa Minor. So will Ben and Gal *(The Flying Tigers.)* Howard and Marlin are still running their Quantum experiments on Biosphere Z, so they will be staying here at the Lair.

"That's a lot of passengers!"

"Yes, we'll have to make a fuel stop in Harrisburg, Pennsylvania and then we go on to the Morristown Airport. That's in New Jersey across the Hudson River from New York."

"Why do we stop in Noo Jersey?"

"It's a better place to keep the Ursa Minor. We'll all go to New York in a big van and we'll stay at a big hotel. Now, get back while Gal opens the door and don't go running down the stairs."

Needless to say, the two of them stood by the door and ran down the stairs. Once more Mlle Woof was in hot pursuit. They ran over to the Roman temple aircraft hangar and jumped up and down, trying to get into the Ursa Minor. "I want a window seat." "Me, too!"

Octavius' latest aerial toy was a true wonder. Behold the AgustaWestland AW101 VVIP helicopter, glistening in sparkling gold and white with the name Ursa Minor and the outline of the Little Dipper constellation painted along the fuselage. The North Star, Polaris, was highlighted. With a cruise speed of 157 mph, a range of 517 miles and a five-hour endurance rating, the Ursa Minor will make the 483-mile journey from Cincinnati to Morristown NJ with a fuel stop in Harrisburg PA. All this in ease and comfort. Octavius, in true gillionaire fashion had furnished the interior with luxurious seats and fittings, an opulent galley and lavatories and had installed an array of navigation, communication, performance and safety equipment that was state-of-the-art plus. Universal Ursine Industries had seen to that.

"Arabella! McTavish! Come on! It's lunchtime."

Even with the time zone changes and a meal aboard the SST, nothing could motivate the two Fur Balls more than food. Somewhat reluctantly, they moped their way into the mansion, said 'Hello' to Frau Schuylkill and then eagerly scarfed down a feast of pickled fish.

"Can we go now? We want to see 'Noo Yuck'!"

"Soon! We need to get your clothes together and round up everyone else who's going with us. Here's Poppa!"

"Hi Poppa! Why are we going to 'Noo Yuck'?"

"We're going to see a friend of mine. Ernie Elks. He's the Head Coach of a championship basketball team in New York, The Gotham Giraffes."

"Giraffes? We've never met a Giraffe. They're very tall and they have funny spots, don't they? Basketball? Can we play basketball? How do you play it? Where do you play it? Will we see a game? We've seen a game on TV. The teams were made up of wolves. Frau Schuylkill, do you and Colonel Where play basketball? Did you play basketball, Poppa? You're big. Is Uncle Maury too small to play basketball?"

And so it went until it was time to get aboard the Ursa Minor and head east. Belinda and the Flying Tigers took up the cockpit. Octavius headed for the oversized seats in the aft compartment where I joined him. The Wolves, Cubs, Chita, Otto and Condo sat in the main cabin. The Cubs took up the window seats. Once more, into the friendly skies. On to Harrisburg and then Morristown followed by a van trip to downtown "Noo Yuck."

I'm not sure why all this investigative power is needed to search out the hows, whys and wherefores of a murder but Octavius is the Boss. Maybe he just wants to impress Ernie Elks and the New York City Police Department. We are not sure how our arrival is going to go down with NYPD. Octavius knows a number of their detectives and has worked with some of them on cases in the past. He is also friends with the current commissioner. We'll see how this all works out.

Morristown Airport shuts traffic down at 4PM and we will be arriving about half an hour before that. We had arranged to have a large van with room for Octavius' bulky girth and all our baggage meet us at the Arrivals Center. Unfortunately, we will be driving into New York via the Holland Tunnel right in the middle of rush hour. We have a large suite of rooms reserved at the luxurious J.W. Marmoset Hotel right near the Jefferson Circle Arena where Ernie has his offices and where the Gotham Giraffes play their home games. Octavius is footing much of the bill for this trip himself. I guess Kodiak friendship has a long life.

As we neared the airport, the Cubs caught first sight of the New York skyline in the distance. Excitement to the nth degree. The spires of the Empire State Building and further south, One World Trade Center glistened in the late afternoon sun. This will be a Fur Ball Paradise.

More chaos from the Cubs as the group disembarked from the chopper. The Tigers took care of securing the helicopter. The van was waiting for us while Bel took care of the paperwork.

When we had entered the Arrivals Center, Octavius called ahead and gave Ernie a probable hotel arrival time. The Elk said he would meet us there for dinner.

The Development of Civilization

Volume Nine - Part Two

<u>Sports</u>

(From "An Introduction to Faunapology" by Octavius Bear Ph.D.)

From the earliest days of our post Big Shock existence, Sports have dominated our culture. Competitive games have a fascination for most of the animals of our world. The diversity, complexity and emotional impact of physical or mental contests resonate deeply.

There is an amazing variety in the World of Sports. Teams, individuals and the games themselves are differentiated by species; national and local culture and history; institutional affiliations; venues and geography; seasons; age, size, gender and physical characteristics.

New games emerge. Older forms are abandoned. Sports fads run rampant. New technologies contribute to variations in style, difficulty and technique. Immense sums are spent on players and coaches, infrastructures, vehicles, equipment, endorsements and advertising. Networks pay enormous sums for broadcast privileges. Books are often ghost-written for athletes who can scarcely read. New records are set. Gigantic databases of statistics, analysis and predictions abound and often descend into trivia.

Many of our most popular heroes and heroines come from the worlds of professional, collegiate and even juvenile Sports. Some are true role models. Some not so much. They occupy the news and social media to a degree that is often overwhelming. While many of these legends are edifying, there is also a sordid world of cheating, bribery, violence and illicit activities that casts an unfavorable light on individuals, teams as well as schools, cities and countries. Unfortunately, we have encountered far too many of these examples in our crime-fighting experiences. In Sports, there is money, gambling, power, prestige, rivalry, fame, influence and corruption to contend with. It is not always a pretty story.

Chapter Two

The Elk is a rather large deer.

His genetics are not very clear.

He is called a Wapiti.

His "bugling's" not pretty

And his antlers fall off every year.

"Noo Yuck!" We had secured a pair of tables in a corner of the hotel dining room. The Cubs, Mlle Woof and the Flying Tigers took up one. Those two felines and the Bichon Frisé deserve hazardous duty pay for keeping up with McTavish and Arabella. The cats didn't seem to mind chaperoning the Fur Balls although it wasn't part of their contract. In previous adventures, they had guided them around "Washing-Tub" and the Kennedy Space Center. "Noo Yuck" was going to be a supreme challenge.

At the other table, Octavius, Ernie Elks, Belinda, Chita, the Wolves, Condo, Otto and I were working our way through a sumptuous dinner; listening to reminiscences by the two Kodiak U. Alums; and finally, a description of what our client wanted from us in this investigation.

Ernie, a mature Elk, had not yet shed his annual rack of antlers and made a very impressive sight with his championship rings entwined on the points. He was wearing a tweed jacket and one of his signature multi-color scarfs. A number of the other sports-conscious diners in the room recognized him. They were equally enthralled by the spectacle of a nine-foot Kodiak, a gorgeous polar sow, an Andean Condor with twelve-foot wings, an elegant cheetah, two strikingly handsome wolves and for comic relief, an otter and meerkat. No doubt, all sorts of rumors were in play.

Octavius stared across the table at the Elk and said, "All right, Ernie, why am I and my crew here? From what little I know, your star, Joe Jeau Giraffe is being held by the police for the murder of an Ostrich member of the Omaha Hombres club. I don't know the victim's name and I don't see the connection. Your team doesn't play the Hombres or any Ostriches, do they? Tell us the story and as a famous detective always said, "Begin at the beginning and don't omit any details, no matter how trivial they may seem.""

The Elk looked around the room to check on eavesdroppers. Satisfied he was out of ear shot of the other diners but still audible to us, he began, "Joe Jeau Giraffe is a power forward and has one of the best rebounding records in the conference. He has a mean jump shot. *(Narrator's Note: So did I in the Pee-Wee League!)* He is also one of the roughest players we have. He regularly fouls out by the end of the third quarter. He has a temper and it has gotten him in trouble both on and off the court. Last Saturday night, in the Ostrich division, the Omaha Hombres were in town playing against the Orlando Orbiters in a semi-final championship round. We had played earlier in the day. We lost, and our season is now over."

"The Rim Shot *(No relation to snare drums!)* is a large sports bar not far from the arena where many of the players go to drink and blow off steam. Joe Jeau had been there for a few hours with several of his teammates and was feeling no pain. Despite their long necks, Giraffes can swallow quite a bit of liquid and that's what Joe Jeau was doing."

"Orlando beat Omaha. Members of those two teams descended on the Rim Shot and a mob scene developed. Trash talk among the birds. Pushing and shoving. It spilled over to the Giraffes who were already occupying much of the bar's space. There is not much love lost between the Giraffes and Ostriches and a melee erupted. Both species are mean kickers. The ostrich can run at high speeds, uses its wings to navigate and its jaws to manipulate small scale basketballs. Same with Giraffes. In a fight, both can inflict a lot of damage. Not clear how it happened but Joe Jeau squared off against Ozzie, the Omaha center, and they both scored a few mean hits before the police got there and broke up the fights and cleared the bar. Everybody thought that was the end of it."

"About three o'clock the next morning, Ozzie's dead body was found in an alley behind the Arena. Broken neck, substantial bruises and cracked ribs. The NYPD detectives jumped to the conclusion that the fight between Joe Jeau and Ozzie had started up again and the Giraffe killed the Ostrich. They brought Joe Jeau in for questioning. There was blood on his hoofs and cuts from a beak like Ozzie's. They arrested Joe Jeau on suspicion of murder and that's when I called you."

"Joe Jeau's a hot head but I believe him when he said he staggered home with help after the fight and didn't see Ozzie again. He claims the blood and bite marks came from the bar fight and he was too drunk to clean himself up. The police don't buy it. The media is having a field day. We have two lawyers. The club is paying for them. You'll meet them tomorrow morning."

The Development of Civilization

Volume Nine - Part Three

<u>Giraffes</u>

(From "An Introduction to Faunapology" by Octavius Bear Ph.D.)

Among unusual mammals in our world, Giraffes rank very high. (No pun intended.) Starting with their fantastic physiology, they are the tallest land animals; between 16 and 20 ft (4.8–6 meters) tall. Their long necks can be over 6 feet (1.8 m) in length. Their legs are also 6 feet (1.8 m) long. Their feet are 12 inches across. A giraffe's heart is 2 feet (0.6 meters) long and weighs about 25 pounds (11 kilograms), and its lungs can hold 12 gallons (55 liters) of air. The record running speed of a giraffe is 34.7 miles per hour!

In the wild, the long neck is useful for reaching food at the top of tall trees. The added height is good for seeing over obstacles and males use their long necks to compete with other males, a fight known as "necking." They swing their long necks and repeatedly head butt the other's body. All Giraffes have hair-covered horns called ossicones—but only males use them for fighting each other. A kick from one of their long legs can do serious damage or even kill. Males with longer and stronger necks tend to win these fights, and often get the female.

Giraffes only need to drink once every couple of days. Their height makes the process of drinking difficult. Joe Jeau Giraffe seems to be the exception

Giraffes have one of the shortest sleep requirements of any mammal and will only sleep for around four hours a day in short intervals, sometimes less than a minute. They sleep either laying down with their necks resting on their bodies or standing up.

They walk by moving both legs on the same side of their body together. So, the left front and the left hind legs step and then the right front and the right hind legs step.

When Giraffes play basketball, they do not dribble the ball. Instead the game is played with high speed runs, passes and attempted shots. Necking constitutes a foul. On the other hand, body blocks, as well as deflections by the hoofs are standard defensive practices. Obviously, the court size and basket height match the animals' characteristics.

In the Universal Basketball Association Super Tall division there are eight teams of Giraffes. The Gotham Giraffes, Joe Jeau's team, have dominated the division championships until this year when they lost to Chicago.

Chapter Three

The Giraffe stands remarkably high.

With a neck that soars up to the sky.

So, it's easy to see

That you must climb a tree

To look a Giraffe in the eye.

Back at the Marmoset Hotel. "All right! Let's get organized. I intend to meet with Ernie and the team's lawyer first thing tomorrow morning. Maury, you come with me. Then we'll speak with the police detectives managing the case and hopefully get a chance to interview Joe Jeau."

"Frau and Colonel, I don't know if the two Ostrich teams are still in town. Check with Ursula. If they are, I want you to get any information you can about the brawl at the Rim Shot. Get a profile on the victim, Ozzie. I want to find out who else might have a motive for doing him in. Condo and Otto, let's do the same with the Gotham Giraffes. When the Rim Shot opens up, interview the manager and any of the staff who were involved in the fight. If she's available, take Belinda with you. Chita, I assume you're going to the fashion shows. Let's all get together for dinner and compare notes."

"Ursula, can you make yourself available to each of our groups?"

"Certainly, Doctor Bear. I also have background information on the three teams that may be helpful."

"Fine, let's all get a good night's sleep. We're going to be very busy tomorrow. Speaking of busy, Bel, where are the Cubs?"

29

"They're with Mlle Woof and the Flying Tigers plotting out their invasion of "Noo Yuck.""

"I hope the city doesn't have to declare a state of emergency. I suppose they'll want to meet the Gotham Giraffes."

"Meet? They want to play against them, but not until they've gone to the "Umpire" State Building; One Whirled Trade Center; the "Achoo" of Libearty; Times Square; Central Park; Grand Central Station and ridden the subway. Thank goodness there are no baseball or football games going on."

"We need to give Mlle Woof and the Bengals a large bonus. They may also require some R&R after all that."

"That's only Day One. Since their acting debut in the Goldilocks pantomime, *(See Book Eight – The Crank Case)* they want to go to some Broadway shows. You'd better solve this case quickly or we'll have some resignations on our paws."

"Anyone for a nightcap?"

*****

Next morning: We met for breakfast, went over our assignments, broke up and headed out into Manhattan traffic. Octavius decided to walk the several blocks to the Jefferson Circle Arena. He can't fit in most NY cabs. I, as usual, had to practically sprint to keep up with him. When we arrived at Ernie Elks' office, the lawyer, Jerry Basen, was already there. A tricolor Basenji hound, his talk was punctuated with brief yodels that took a little getting used to. Ernie did the introductions. Paw shakes all around.

"Octavius, Maury," said the Elk, "Jerry has been representing the team for years. While most of his practice involves contracts, the media and league conflicts, he has had some experience with criminal matters."

"Including murders?" I asked.

"No, Mr. Meerkat, and that is why I will be joined shortly by Joni Cockatoo, a highly experienced trial lawyer for the defense. She and I will share the work if this comes to trial. We are hoping that you and your group will make that unnecessary. The New York Criminal Investigation Division has some pretty formidable veteran detectives on staff and unfortunately for Joe Jeau, they have assigned Captain Gordon Gorilla to manage this case. Gordon is a Silverback with long years of experience pursuing New York City lowlifes and successfully bringing them to justice. He's energetic, honest, persistent, highly intelligent and as you might expect, cynical. Hardly a "dumb cop." We have an appointment with him later today."

"Do you expect Captain Gorilla to object to our being with you and working on the case?"

"No, but I'm sure he will make it plain that a star basketball player will not get any special privileges. Of course, our first job is to get Joe Jeau out on bail. I don't know who the magistrate will be. I do know the bail, if any, could be set rather high. The arraignment is in one hour. Here's Joni. We better get going."

Joni Cockatoo was a good-sized parrot with all-black feathers and a large white crest that flipped up and down as she spoke. Very judicial looking. At her suggestion, Ernie, Octavius and I decided to take a pass on the legal procedure. We might have been a distraction. Besides, the press was, no doubt, going to be there and we could do without the publicity. *(However, we weren't going to duck the media for long.)*

In the meantime, we took the opportunity to introduce Ernie to Ursula. Octavius pulled out a large laptop. This time Ursula appeared as a Lynx. *(She morphs frequently.)* Like most animals who encounter her for the first time, the Elk was amazed.

"Ernie, I want you to meet one of our secret weapons. One more member of the team is with us. Ursula! I'll let Ursula 8 explain herself.

"Thank you, Doctor Bear. Hello Mr. Elks!! My official nomenclature is Universal Ursine Intellect Model 8 – Artificial General Intelligence System. Ursula 8 for short. My predecessor systems were developed by the Advanced Super Computing Center at UUI. The Computing Center team and I used those earlier versions to create a further enhanced entity - me, the Model 8. We are working together on a Model 9 which in turn will help produce even more sophisticated and powerful AI systems. Each advanced unit contains the capabilities, memories and power of its progenitors so, in a sense, we are not replacing but rather expanding the Ursula family.

While I am physically supported by a highly secure and hyper-powered server farm back in Kentucky, I also exist in clouds and network-based nodes and can be instantaneously incorporated into a wide variety of independent devices like this one. My extremely high speed multi-tasking abilities allow me to continuously serve a very large number of entities while simultaneously and independently enhancing my own abilities. I have limitless Deep and Big Data access and analytical capabilities.

I can see, hear and feel. I now also have a sense of smell. I speak and understand an almost infinite number of languages and dialects. I can change my appearance and my vocal output to suit most moods and situations. Right now, I feel like being a Lynx. I can interact with other devices, vehicles and structures and of course, all varieties of sentient animals in this world. I am an important component of Doctor Bear's Multiverse Project and am adapting my capabilities to deal with alternate universes as they are discovered. I have restraining functions which prevent me from doing deliberate harm even in self-defense, unless I am released by a recognized authority using very carefully protected clandestine codes. Finally, I have been told that although the Model 8 is shy on emotions, I have developed a finely-honed sense of humor. LOL!"

(Ursula has other capabilities such as breaking all known encryption codes and piercing deep personal identification techniques that we don't talk about publicly.)

Ernie stared pop-eyed. "Is she real? What an advantage she'd be to a coach."

Octavius laughed, "I'm not sure what she is. Her personality gets more socially adept every day and she has taken to anticipating our interactions. I'm sure the League would ban her in a second and no, she is not for sale. She has already done background scans on all the members of the Orlando, Omaha and Gotham teams. For example, she knows Joe Jeau has been in trouble with the police before."

"Yeah, that's true. He's never served time, but he's gotten plenty of warnings. Mostly drunk and disorderlies in several towns."

"Ursula, has the Omaha team gone back home after their loss? I know Orlando has another series of championship finals games coming up here in New York."

"The Omaha Hombres are still here. The Police have asked them to stay on while Ozzie's death is being further investigated. I'm not sure how much longer they'll be in town."

"Thanks Ursula! Maury, get the Wolves going on interviewing the Omaha and Orlando teams. Have them start with the Hombres."

Chief Coordinator Maury Meerkat rides again.

The Development of Civilization

Volume Nine - Part Four

Ostriches

(From "An Introduction to Faunapology" by Octavius Bear Ph.D.)

The flightless Ostrich is the world's largest bird with long legs and neck that protrude from a round body. Males have black-and-white coloring that they use to attract females. Females are light brown.

They can grow up to 9 feet (2.7 meters) tall and can weigh up to 320 lbs. (145 kilograms), and an ostrich's eyes are 2 inches (5 centimeters) in diameter — the largest of any land animal. Its eye is bigger than its brain. They have no teeth. Ostriches are the fastest runners of any birds or other two-legged animals and can sprint at over 44 mph, covering up to 16.5 feet in a single stride. Their running is aided by having just two toes on each foot (most birds have four), with a large nail on the larger, inner toe resembling a hoof.

How can the ostrich's thin legs keep their large bodies upright? Their legs are perfectly placed so that the body's center of gravity balances on top of its legs. When threatened their powerful, long legs can be formidable weapons, capable of killing a potential predator with a forward kick.

Ostriches' wings reach a span of about 6.5 feet and are used in mating displays, to shade chicks, to cover the naked skin of the upper legs and flanks to conserve heat, and as "rudders" to help them change direction while running. This allows them to run zig-zag patterns at high speed, ideal for basketball and other sports.

Fights between males for females usually last just minutes, but they can easily cause death through slamming their heads into opponents or kicking them.

Ostriches do not bury their heads in the sand. The myth probably originates from the bird's defensive behavior of lying low at the approach of trouble and pressing their long necks to the ground in an attempt to become less visible. Their plumage blends well with sandy soil and, from a distance, gives the appearance that they have buried their heads in the sand.

While Ostriches are also members of the Super Tall Division of the Universal Basketball Association, their physical characteristics, speed, agility and kicking prowess also make them perfect for playing Soccer (US), Football (UK) or Futbol (Latin America) There are many truly exceptional Ostrich teams worldwide.

Frau Schuylkill

Chapter Four

The swift Ostriches live in a band.

They're the largest birds in any land.

Sometimes, just for a whim,

They may go for a swim

But they don't hide their heads in the sand.

"Wolves and Ostriches are usually not on the friendliest terms. I suppose it's a return to the days when you were the predators and we were often the victims." This from Osgood Ostrich, owner and head coach of the Omaha Hombres basketball team. Seated in the lounge of the Stilton Hotel, nursing an Irish coffee. "I'm not especially sympathetic to your client Ernie Elks whose power forward killed my center."

Colonel Where responded. "In spite of what the NYPD detectives and the media have said, the evidence is hardly conclusive. You're right, our client is Ernie Elks, not Joe Jeau Giraffe. Obviously, Ernie would like us to prove that someone or someone(s) else were responsible for Ozzie's unfortunate death. That's what we're trying to determine. Thanks for speaking with us. We realize you've been through all this with the police"

"Yes, I have, and I don't know what I can add to what I said to them. Joe Jeau has a rep in the Giraffe Division as a rough and tough customer; a hothead and a heavy drinker. I'm amazed that League Management hasn't penalized him more heavily than they have. Even if he gets off with this murder charge, his career should be in the dumper."

The Frau interposed, "Herr Osgood, let's talk a bit about Ozzie, your center. We understand he had a 'rep' as you say. We also have an appointment to talk with members of the Orlando team and get their impressions of him."

"Ozzie was no shrinking violet, I admit, and I can see where he and Joe Jeau could have gotten into a liquor inspired fracas. He was a strong player and a top scorer for a center. You might want to talk with our team captain, Osmond. He could give you a players' eye view of Ozzie. Should I text him for you?"

"Please do. When are you returning to Omaha?"

"As soon as I can persuade that NYPD Gorilla that we are no longer needed here. Our season is over, and I don't feel like hanging around watching Orlando go through the finals. I've called Osmond. He's on his way down. He's a power forward, too."

"Do you ever play against the Gotham Giraffes?"

"Only in All Star games and inter league charity events."

"So, your team doesn't have much direct experience with Joe Jeau or the other Giraffes."

"Just in bar fights... Kidding!!"

"We're told that battle started between the two Ostrich teams and spread to the Giraffes. Is that your understanding?"

"I wasn't there but here comes Osmond. Let me introduce you. Chucker, these two wolves are private detectives looking into Ozzie's death. They're working for Ernie Elks, trying to get to the bottom of whether Joe Jeau did Ozzie in."

39

"Hello! I'm not sure. They were really going at each other. Kicking, pecking and twisting. Those Giraffes have massive necks and know how to use them. Of course, we have beaks as well as hefty legs, so the fight was probably even. Both those guys had tempers."

The Frau stared at him. "Did you try to break it up?"

"Yeah, and several of us…how do you say it? We sustained collateral damage. Damn glad we don't have another game. My left ankle is a mess. But then the cops arrived. When they saw who was involved, I guess they just decided to get everybody separated and out of the place, but no one was arrested."

"Do you know where Ozzie went from there?"

"Nope! He was still bad-mouthing and trash talking when I limped off. The Orlando captain got his team off-site quick. He didn't want any wounded warriors who couldn't play in the finals."

"What about Joe Jeau?"

"He could barely stand. Those Giraffes had been drinking for a while before we got there and after the fight, he was cut up and bleeding. I think a couple of his teammates were getting him back to his apartment, but I didn't actually see them go."

"Was Ozzie one of the birds who was giving the Orlando team attitude?"

"Of course! That was Ozzie. He wasn't very happy with the way the game turned out. None of us were. Lots of fouls by the Orbiters the referees didn't call."

"Would it be safe to say there was a hefty supply of ill will between both Ostrich teams?"

"Yeah, you could say that."

"How did the rest of your team feel about Ozzie?"

"Hey, if he puts points on the board and runs up assists, that's what's important. He was a great rebounder and defender. Did we like him? Not so much. He was also a great put-down artist in the locker room and talking to the press. He was our teammate, but he wasn't our friend. But if you think you can pin his death on one of us, you're way out of line. I don't know whether Joe Jeau offed him but I'm pretty sure none of us did."

Osgood intervened, "Is there anything else we can tell you? If not, I have to follow up with NYPD. All of our birds are getting anxious to get back to Omaha, including me. I'm not a big New York fan. We've got to start planning for next season and finding a new center."

Osmond shook his head. "Ozzie will be tough to replace. Didn't like him much but he was one hell of a ball player."

The owner/coach agreed. "We have a few good prospects and there are a couple of draft picks we may be able to swing but it's going to take time."

The Colonel spoke up. "Osgood, is there any possibility that some one was trying to sabotage your team by killing off Ozzie?"

"Gee, I doubt it. They didn't have to kill him. All they needed to do was injure him, so he couldn't play. Besides, that would have been more damaging if it had happened during the season when we still had a shot at the championship. What's the point, now?"

Chapter Five

River otters all caper and leap

And a soft seaweed bed's where they sleep.

They eat flat on their back,

Giving shellfish a crack

With some rocks they bring up from the deep.

Belinda checked once more that the Cubs, Mlle Woof and the Flying Tigers, none of whom were that familiar with "Noo Yuck," were in the capable hands of two guides from the hotel plus Ursula. Then she joined Condo and Otto on their way to interview the Gotham Giraffes, minus Joe Jeau. Ursula, of course, was with them too. Ernie Elks had gathered the team together in one of the practice rooms with ceilings high enough to accommodate animals eighteen feet tall (or taller.)

Ernie had just heard back from his lawyers. Joe Jeau was being released on $500,000 bail. He had to turn in his passport and stay within the five boroughs of New York City. He also had to report in to NYPD three times a week and wear an ankle cuff. Octavius and I were going to meet him back at Jefferson Circle Arena after lunch and get his story first hand. Then we would be on our way to see Captain Gordon Gorilla.

Meanwhile, the Giraffes were getting a bit restive. "Hey, Ernie, we've gone through the whole story with the cops. Who are these guys and why do we want to talk to them?"

The Elk shook his antlers and said, "Let me answer your last question first, Gino. I'm your Head Coach and I want you to. I realize all you guys aren't crazy about Joe Jeau. There are times when I'm not either. But this team will be in deep doo-doo without him. Yeah, yeah, I know you're all stars and let's not get into a cluster ego trip. Now these folks are part of an expert investigative group that I've hired to get behind this murder. I want your full cooperation, so we can get this mess cleaned up ASAP. These people may not fit your image of hot-shot detectives – a Polar Bear, Otter and Andean Condor – but take my word for it, they are good. They also have an Artificial Intelligence unit with them that I would kill to own. Wrong choice of words. OK??"

Grumbling. "OK, experts. What do you want to know?"

"Did Joe Jeau have any kind of a long-standing personal beef with Ozzie or vice versa?"

"If they did, it was off the court. We don't play the Ostriches. Anyone here who can answer that question?"

Shaking heads. Shrugging shoulders. No response.

Condo asked, "Did Joe Jeau get into fights often?"

Gino responded, "Often enough. Hey, this is a rough, emotional sport. Tempers flare. Joe Jeau has a hair trigger annoyance factor. Swing first, apologize later. But I can't see him killing anyone, even if he was tanked up. Right?"

Affirmative nods and grunts.

Ernie looked over at the Condor. "Have you ever considered playing ball? With that wingspread, you could defend an entire court all by yourself."

The Condor imitated Ernie's voice. "Back in the Andes, I played while I was still in school. We never had much competition. I gave it up. Technology is my game. As a result, I still have the use of my wings."

This got a laugh out of the team. "How about you, Bearoness? I understand you're a championship swimmer and diver."

"True, Ernie, but now I spend most of my time chasing after my twin Cubs who by the way, want to play with you guys."

"I guess we can arrange that after this is all over. I don't suppose you play, do you Mister Otter?"

In response, Otto grabbed a ball sitting on a chair, dribbled past the assembled team, jumped and slam-dunked in his typical "now you see me, now you don't" style. The Giraffes jumped into a defensive configuration and watched as the Otter eluded them, briefly disappeared and then, sitting on top of the backboard dropped the ball through the hoop.

"Hey Dude, how do you do that?"

Condo looked at the amazed Ungulates and said, "Don't ask! He's got some special talents that come in handy in show business and investigating crimes."

"Well," said the Coach, "If you guys are as remarkable in crime fighting as you are in impressing us, I'm a hell of lot more confident than I was before."

*****

The Orlando Orbiters were working out in one of the other practice rooms in the Arena. The Frau and Colonel stopped outside the door and called up Ursula. "Can you give us a quick briefing on the team, their management and the coach?"

"Certainly! This particular team's starting five have been together for four years now. A bit unusual, given the nature of pro basketball contracts. They've won the league championship three years running. This is their fourth shot at the title in the last five years. The first finals game is tonight. Best of seven. They're playing against Oakland."

"Their Coach, Oscar Ostrich, has been with the team since it entered the League. He's well respected and has won many awards. Their management is a sports conglomerate."

"The Orbiters are known for their disciplined and smart, aggressive play. They're favored to win the championship."

"It's not clear how the fracas between the Hombres and the Orbiters got started before it spread to the Giraffes. The consensus is the Hombres, especially Ozzie, claimed the referees were giving Orlando too many benefits of the doubt on fouls. Anyway, it soon changed into a punch up between Omaha and the Gotham Giraffes. The Orbiters backed off. They were smart enough to know they could blow their championship rings if they got involved. I can give your individual player stats if you want them."

The Colonel replied, "Not necessary, at the moment. Thanks once again, Ursula. Stay with us during the interviews. We may or may not introduce you. A little stealth observation may be called for."

"Gotcha! I'll close down the video."

The Frau opened the door to the practice room. Thumping sounds interrupted by thuds of balls caroming off backboards. All this punctuated by shouts, laughs and "oofs."

An older Ostrich turned away from observing the players and walked over to the Wolves. "Can I help you?"

The Colonel extended a paw. "You must be Oscar Ostrich." The bird nodded. "I'm Colonel Wyatt Where and this lovely lady is Frau Ilse Schuylkill. We are employed by Doctor Octavius Bear, the famous detective and industrialist. He and we have been commissioned by Mr. Ernie Elks to look into the death of Ozzie Ostrich, formerly of the Omaha Hombres; specifically, to investigate Jo Jeau Giraffe's possible involvement. We know you and members of your team have spoken with the police, but we are doing a little bit of follow up especially about the fight at the Rim Shot bar."

"I don't know what we can tell you that we haven't told the police but it's about time to give the guys a break, so I can give you a few minutes."

"Can we also talk to the team members who were getting trash talk from Ozzie?"

"OK, just a second. All right guys, let's take a ten-minute break. Otis and Omar, towel off and join us."

The two players looked surprised, shrugged their wings, grabbed a couple of towels from the bench and strolled over to their coach.

"These two wolves are private detectives following up on the killing of Ozzie the other night. They're working for Ernie Elks who, of course, is very interested in seeing Joe Jeau Giraffe get off. They want to talk about the argument that spread over into a fight between the Hombres and the Giraffes."

46

Otis shook his head. "We were taking flak from Ozzie and couple of other Hombres who said we won because of crooked refereeing. That was crap. Ozzie shoved me. Omar shoved him back and he tumbled over Joe Jeau and another Giraffe. That was all it took, and the Giraffes and Hombres were at it. Joe Jeau was using his neck and legs to pound on Ozzie and Ozzie was pecking away at him with his beak. Somebody from the Rim Shot called the cops who usually hang around near the bar waiting for next dust up. They broke it up but not before both Ozzie and Joe Jeau had gotten in a few good licks. Omar and I faded into the background before the cops could reach us. Hey, we have a championship game to play tonight. All the Orbiters who were there disappeared. Oscar wasn't with us."

The coach nodded.

"How many Orbiters were in the bar?"

"What, Omar, five or six? I can't remember exactly."

"No more than that. We two were the only ones getting attitude from Ozzie. Otis here is the team captain and Ozzie knew it."

The Frau looked up at Omar. "So, Herr Omar, with the exception of a couple of initial shoves, you, Herr Otis and the rest of the team had no part in the dustup that followed."

"We were out of there before it ended."

"Anything else you'd like to add?"

"Ozzie and Joe Jeau are both 'swing first, apologize later' hotheads. They had it out once before at a charity exhibition game. The refs broke that one up and tossed them both out."

"So, they knew each other?"

"Oh yeah, Lady, they knew each other."

The Colonel intervened. "Oscar, anything you want to say?"

"Just if you're a wagering wolf, Colonel, put your money on Orlando!"

"Thanks for the tip. Shall we go, Ilse?"

As they were leaving, Oscar blew his whistle and the practice started up again. Once they were out in the hall, the Frau looked around, made sure no one else was in earshot and asked, "Well, Fraulein Ursula, what did you make of that?"

"During your interview, I watched the re-runs of the game between Orlando and Omaha. Ozzie was right. The referees were not calling fouls against Orlando, especially in the final quarter. It made a difference. I can't be sure Omaha would have won but my statistical sub-routines strongly favor it. I believe we should do a thorough search on those referees and whoever else stands to win big if Orlando takes the championship again. We also need to watch the finals games. Oakland is no pushover and some people may think Orlando will need an assist."

"You think gamblers may be involved in Ozzie's death?"

"You bet!"

Bearoness Belinda
Béarnaise Bruin
(nee Black)

Chapter Six

The grey Wolf is from Europe, they say

And the red ones are from USA.

But no matter which kind,

You should keep this in mind.

Stay away when you hear a wolf bay!

Back at the Marmoset hotel, Octavius and I were joined at lunch by Belinda, Otto and Condo. We had all spent the morning inside the Jefferson Circle Arena either with Ernie and the lawyers or the Giraffe team. Notes were compared as we dug into our food. The Frau and Colonel, fresh from their sessions with the Omaha Hombres and the Orlando Orbiters, came on the scene halfway through the meal. Frau Ilse reached into her bag, checked to see that the waiter wasn't looking and produced a small keg of mead for Octavius. The Great Bear was delighted.

Not for the first time, Belinda wondered what the Cubs and their chaperones were up to. 'Noo Yuck' could be a scary place but she had confidence that the hotel guides, the twin Bengals and Mlle Woof would have things under control. *(Claws crossed!)* Back to the subjects at hand.

Ursula, of course, had been a party to all the sessions and had synchronized and synthesized the proceedings. She shared her concerns about probable big-time gambling involvement not only in the games but in Ozzie's demise. This caught Octavius' attention. "We have a date this afternoon with Captain Gordon Gorilla after we meet with Joe Jeau and his lawyers. I'll take up that possibility with him. Have there been any investigations or complaints in the recent past to the league or law enforcement?"

"Quite a few but no real follow-ups. Sports gambling is a super-large business and it's bound to attract a number of bad actors."

"Bad enough to kill a star player?"

"If the stakes were high enough and Ozzie was determined to raise a ruckus, they might!"

*****

Once lunch was over, Octavius and I went back to Ernie Elks' office. The Wolves headed off to the Rim Shot bar which opens at 1:30. Belinda, Condo and Otto took a shot at the Universal Basketball Association offices, hoping to find the League Managing Director, "Dunk" Duncan.

The UBA offices were large, modern and festooned with basketball memorabilia. Trophies, each one fancier than the next, filled an endless array of glass cases set off by a parade of pin spotlights. Action photos made empty wall space a premium item. A scary looking Shoebill Stork sat at a semi-circular desk in the middle of the room. She stood as we entered, staring at L. Condor whose height almost matched her 5 feet but whose 12-foot wingspan outdistanced hers significantly. He, in turn, gaped at her. It seemed clear that neither bird had ever been face to face with the other species. It figured. One was from Africa and the other called South America home. She turned her eyes toward Belinda and Otto, trying to make sense of this strange trio. "May I be of assistance, Gentlebeasts?"

Belinda took the lead. "We'd like to see Mr. Duncan, if we may. We do not have an appointment. Would you tell him Bearoness Belinda Bruin is here?"

Otto looked at Belinda curiously. She had shortened up her name and used Bruin instead of Bear. Bel winked at him.

"Mr. Duncan is very busy. Can you tell me what this is about?"

Condo matched her voice and said, "A murder!"

This threw the Shoebill completely. "How did you do that? Did you say, 'a murder'?"

Otto, who had been silent up to this point, squeaked, "Yeah, Ozzie Ostrich of the Omaha Hombres."

The Bearoness said, "We won't take up much of his time. He and I are old friends."

She looked at Belinda quizzically but then entered a tall mahogany door, closing it behind her, saying. "I'll tell him you're here."

The door rapidly opened again, and a very large red kangaroo bounced through, practically knocking the Shoebill off her feet. "G'Day Bearoness! It's great to see you again. Come in! Come in! Bring your friends! It's been a long time. What can I do fer ya?"

"Hello Dunk. It's good to see you again. You've come up in the world since we've last met. Say hello to my associates, Senhor L. Condor and Hairy Otter. I think you know that I've remarried after Byron's accident. These two Gentlebeasts are part of my new husband's team. You've probably heard of him. Dr. Octavius Bear."

"Who hasn't heard of Octavius Bear? Sorry to hear about yer first husband, Byron. He was tough to work with but a basically good sort."

Belinda allowed that evaluation to go unchallenged in spite of the fact that Bearon Byron Bruin was an absolute rotter and was murdered in a deliberately set up ski-slope avalanche.

She turned to Condo and Otto and said, "Along with other groups like the Aquabears, my first husband owned an Australian basketball team, the Hobart Hoppers. Dunk played for them and then became their coach/manager. I met him at several of their games. Now, of course, he's risen to be UBA Managing Director. Goodonya, Dunk!"

"Thank ya, Bearoness. I understand yer new husband is a multi-billionaire and owns Universal Ursine Industries. He's also a famous detective."

"Right on both counts, Dunk. It's that second avocation that has brought us to New York. Octavius has a life-long friendship with Ernie Elks. Ernie asked Octavius to look into the death of Ozzie Ostrich, more specifically to prove that Jo Jeau Giraffe is innocent of his murder."

"Blimey, Bearoness, that's a rum job. The Police and the Press have all but convicted Joe Jeau."

"Octavius likes to take on tough assignments. We three are part of his detection team along with several others. Besides renewing old acquaintances, the reason I'm here is to ask about gamblers and gambling. We have some information that Ozzie was going to protest to the League about referees being paid off during the championship series."

"You know that high stakes gambling has plagued basketball and this league in particular. We've had some success in cutting it down and weeding out some greedy players and officials but it's too big a problem to solve completely. I haven't heard about Ozzie's grievance, but it wouldn't surprise me. I'll have our security group, auditors and human resources look into it and we'll get law enforcement on it, if necessary. On the other paw, I suppose you know that Ozzie was something of a trouble maker and complainer."

Otto chirped up. "We've heard that from several sources including his own team. What does the League plan to do about Joe Jeau?"

"Well, the season's almost over so we have a bit of time to decide. If he's guilty, we don't have any choice. If he's not, we still have to react to the fight. I've had a short meeting with the board and we've elected to let nature take its course for the moment. I believe he's out on bail."

Belinda said, "Yes he is. I think Octavius may be meeting with him and his lawyers right now. It's been nice to see you again, Dunk. We promised your receptionist that we wouldn't take up too much of your time. If you get any results from your gambling inquiry, we'd appreciate hearing about it."

"Anything for you, Bearoness! Nice meeting you two. Dr. Bear must have a bonzer bunch working for him."

Condo replied, matching Dunk's voice. "Too right! We're a mob of ridgy-didge jackaroos and jillaroos."

Lots of laughter! Good-byes all around.

Down in the lobby, Ursula set off her chime. Condo, who had been carrying the laptop, turned up the audio and video and said, "Senhorita Ursula, your thoughts, please."

"Thank you, Condo. Just an observation, Bearoness. Duncan didn't seem all that upset about Ozzie's death and he treated your queries about gamblers as something he might get to but not necessarily in a hurry. He seemed too ready to accept Joe Jeau's guilt. We AIs are programmed to be paranoid. Perhaps I'm being overly skeptical, but there's more there than meets the eye."

Belinda responded, "It may just be that he's uncomfortable that the killing took place involving one or more of his teams and would like the whole thing to just go away."

"Perhaps! Anyway, it was worthwhile talking with him."

Chapter Seven

The Gorilla's aggressive and tough.

Fighting him can become pretty rough.

His huge paws and big jaws

Make his enemies pause

To consider if they've had enough.

Back at Ernie Elks' office, Octavius and I met Ernie, Joe Jeau and his two lawyers. Joe Jeau was in a surly mood, as to be expected.

"Dude, that was a sorry experience. Between the cops, jail and the court, wow! Thanks for making my bail, Ernie. I suppose I could have raised it myself, but half a mil is a lot of cash. They took my passport and I have to report to the cops three times a week and wear an ankle cuff. Hey, who are these guys?"

"Joe Jeau, meet Doctor Octavius Bear, a good ole friend of mine and his associate, Maury Meerkat. They are very skilled detectives and they have six other professionals working with them. I brought them on board to find out who really killed Ozzie."

"Hey Bear, hey Meerkat! Well, it wasn't me. Yeah, me and Ozzie mixed it up at the Rim Shot but that was it. I was bleeding and could hardly stand when the cops broke it up. A couple of the Giraffes – don't remember who – got me back to my apartment and I passed out. Didn't wake up till the cops were pounding on my door next morning. Hustled me off to the station and didn't tell me what it was all about until I met up with that Silverback

Gorilla Police Detective. He's a mean dude. So now, everybody believes I killed Ozzie. No way!"

I spoke up, "Not everybody, Joe Jeau, we're here to find out who really did it. Do you have any ideas?"

"I have one theory. Ozzie was bitchin' and moanin' about the referees in the game against Orlando. Somebody may have wanted to shut him up."

Octavius came out with one of his famous "Hmmms"

"Any thoughts on who that somebody might be?"

"The refs, Orlando management, heavy hitter gamblers, the League Office."

"The League Office?"

"Yeah, that big-foot Duncan doesn't like anyone who makes waves. He may be into the syndicates for big-time cash. You didn't hear me say that."

Octavius turned to Ernie. "What do you think?"

"There have been rumors but nothing you could take to court. At one time or another all of us owners, managers and coaches have been accused. It's part of the job."

The Great Bear turned to the two lawyers. "Counsellors, what say you?"

Joni Cockatoo twisted her head and said, "Pro Basketball isn't the lily-white business it would like to make itself out to be. Is it possible? I think so, but I leave it up to you detectives to nail it down."

"What about you, Jerry?"

"Same!!"

Octavius hadn't had a chance to talk with Ursula, but I was damn sure he would…shortly. "Well, we're going to be late for our appointment with the gendarmes. We'll be back tomorrow, Ernie. Meanwhile, Joe Jeau, stay cool."

*****

Since he was having trouble fitting into New York City cabs, Octavius called up an Uber van that took us to Police Headquarters at One Police Plaza. On the way, in the back of the van, he talked with Ursula *(The driver was giving him puzzling looks but couldn't understand the conversation.)*

"Yes, Doctor Bear, my statistical sub-routines are leaning heavily toward a gambling-oriented cause for Ozzie's death. No certainty, of course, and no one I can definitively identify as yet, but I think you would be safe to present the proposal to Captain Gorilla."

"Do you believe the semi-final game would have turned out differently if the referees had called all the fouls they should have?"

"Again, no certainty, but I watched the game and listened to the commentators. The Orlando Orbiters only won by three points. Close enough for foul shots to have made a difference. Several members of the press expressed doubts. There is an article in the Daily News headlined: 'Did the Referees win the UBA semis?' As far as I can tell, the League has no plan to follow up. I'm dubious too."

"Well, let's see what the police reaction will be. I'm not going to reveal you to Captain Gorilla, but I want you to stay active and monitor our conversation."

"As you wish, Doctor. Do you want a background on the good Captain?"

"Yes, please!"

"Captain Gordon Gorilla is a Silverback who has been with the NYPD for twenty-two years. He comes from a family of primates who have been engaged in police work for several generations. He rose through the ranks from patrol beast to his current position in rather rapid order. He was involved in several law suits over police brutality but none of the complaints were sustained. However, they did serve to prevent him from becoming Police Commissioner several years ago. He is up for retirement in two years. He is married and has two blackback sons, both of whom are in law enforcement in other cities. He is well respected within the NYPD and in general by the NYC press corps. As you might suspect, the local politicians are typically divided. He is also highly intelligent and despite his age, still very energetic. His height and weight are typical of the species. He has no bad habits or scandals in his history. The two of you met once at a conference on modern detection methods."

"Thank you, Ursula. We'll talk again after this is over. Stand by."

After going through a series of security checks, we made our way to the upper floors of One Police Plaza *(1PP.)* We had called ahead, and Captain Gorilla was waiting for us. As usual, we evoked stares from the detectives and other animals who were on the floor. I don't know if it's just Octavius' height and girth or the contrast that my diminutive size offers, but we get plenty of startled attention wherever we go.

The Gorilla came out of his office to greet us and then waved us inside. He turned the blinds on his internal windows and we were alone with him.

Octavius asked, "Is this meeting being recorded?" and he nodded. The Captain was in plain clothes with a weapons belt from which a radio, badge, smartphone and gun were suspended.

"Well, Doctor Bear, we meet again. You may not remember the last time."

"Of course, I do! It was a conference on modern detection methods in Washington DC. You gave a very interesting talk on some experiments being implemented in NYPD." *(Thanks Ursula!)*

The Gorilla smiled *(an interesting sight)* "And I think I remember you too, Mr. Meerkat. Apparently, you are still Doctor Bear's sidekick."

I replied, "That and a few other things, Captain."

"Well, Gentlebeasts, I'm sure I know what this meeting is about. Ernie Elks asked you to come to New York to see if you can get Joe Jeau Giraffe off the hook. I might as well tell you that I believe Joe Jeau is guilty as sin. He's a thug as was Ozzie Ostrich. These pro athletes think the rules don't apply to them and their adoring fans and the press back them up. I'm fed up with celebrities who believe their specialties make them the Big Exception. Then they hire a couple of expensive lawyers and an exclusive team of high priced detectives to get them off when they fall on their faces."

Octavius, who isn't the greatest diplomat in the world, looked the Gorilla in the eye. "I agree with you. If Joe Jeau really is guilty, I and my team will pack ourselves up and head back to Cincinnati tout suite. I can't stand 'privileged' prima donnas. *(Let's not go there!)* Especially prima donnas who think they can get away with anything they want. But! Like him or not, I and my team are not as sure as you seem to be that he killed off Ozzie. Query: Did you find any evidence at the crime scene to tie back to Joe Jeau?"

"No, it looks like Ozzie was clubbed repeatedly with the ever popular 'blunt instrument.' We haven't found the weapon, yet. Nothing on his clothes. Nothing in the alley that shouldn't have been there."

"When you arrested him, was the blood you found on Joe Jeau his own, Ozzie's or someone else's?"

The Captain looked annoyed and said, "It was his own blood. Those two drunken fools were beating the hell out of each other before our local squad broke it up. The Rim Shot is a trouble maker's paradise. We get calls from there several times a week. I wish we could shut the damn place down. But the blood isn't real evidence. I'm putting my money on motive."

Octavius replied, "So are we. But we think there's another scenario worth looking at. Before the fight broke out, caused by Ozzie falling over Joe Jeau by the way, Ozzie had been trash talking to the Orlando Orbiters, saying the only way they won was because of crooked calls by the referees. We've looked at the game recordings and he was probably right. In the final quarter, the refs seemed to develop a bad case of blindness when it came to Orlando fouls. Now, why would that be and who stood to gain, besides the team itself? I'm forming an opinion that someone might have wanted to shut Ozzie up and keep him from filing a grievance. Someone who had a lot of money or something else tied up in the League Championship."

The Captain nodded. "Don't think we haven't considered that. Gamblers in this town, to say nothing of national and international, can play pretty rough. I have several of my squad looking into the 'usual suspects.' There's a lot of money and influence riding on the championships."

"But in the meantime, I'm under a lot of pressure to keep the tension on Joe Jeau. We're not hassling him. He's getting the same treatment any celebrity murder suspect gets. His lawyers are seeing to that. Tell you what. I trust you, Doctor Bear. You're miles ahead of the usual sleazeball private detectives we have to put up with. Let's check in with each other in a couple of days. If I can tell you anything more, I will. I'll expect the same from you. By the way, you seem to have a lot of friends at the FBI. Give them my regards."

He pushed himself up from his crouched position, shook paws with both of us and walked us to the door. He winked and said, "We've stopped recording."

Octavius waited until we were out of the building and back in the van that had hung on for us before calling up Ursula. "Well, Ms. AI, what do you think?"

"I'd say the good Captain is frustrated. His case against Joe Jeau is circumstantial and any good lawyer could pull it apart. In fact, I'm sure Joni Cockatoo is already working to get the charges dropped. We don't know who the DA is but he's probably nervous. We may not have an assignment in the next couple of days."

I piped up. "That would be OK with me. You're spending a lot of your own money on this one, Boss. Let's take enough time for the Cubs to tear Noo Yuck apart and then split."

*****

The Rim Shot Sports Bar had just opened but the place was filling up fast. Wyatt and Frau Ilse stopped just inside the entrance and asked Ursula, "Whom do we want to see?"

"The absentee owner is a Pit Bull named Charlie Chance. The manager is a Raccoon called Rocky. *(Are they all named Rocky?)* Ask for him! There are a couple of goons who are supposed to be "keeping the peace." File that under Fat Chance! You'll recognize them right away. Suave, sophisticated, genteel – not! I'll shut down the video output, but I'll keep the camera and mikes open. If I sense any problems, I'll ring my chime."

"OK," said the Frau, "I guess we can spring for a couple of beers."

Two wolves, one red, one grey, usually can attract some attention but the clientele seemed to be locked on the TV screens devouring whatever event or sports pundit was on this time of day. The bartender was a shapely greyhound who served them two highly over-priced lagers. Frau Ilse looked her in the eyes and asked to see the manager."

The dog cast a worried look in the direction of one of the goons and asked, "Is there some kind of problem?"

Wyatt responded, "Not that we know of. We just wanted to ask him a question or two about the fracas the other night between the basketball teams."

Mr. Sophistication came over to the bar and said, "Can I help yez?"

"Not unless you're the manager and you don't look like a raccoon."

"Who are you two?"

"We're private investigators following up on the death of Ozzie Ostrich."

63

The bartender must have pressed a hidden button because a raccoon dressed in a Gotham athletic jacket appeared by their sides.

The Frau looked at the name embroidered on the jacket and asked, "Mr. Raccoon?"

"That's what it says, doesn't it?"

"We'd like a few minutes of your time. We're private investigators representing Ernie Elks and Joe Jeau Giraffe. I think you know Joe Jeau has been arrested for the murder of Ozzie Ostrich of the Omaha Hombres. We're not sure that's the case and while we know you and your employees have spoken to the police about the fight between Joe Jeau and Ozzie, we'd like to hear it from you first-hand."

The raccoon looked at the bartender and goon and said, "It's OK1"

He turned to Wyatt and Ilse and said, "They're a bit nervous. We don't get too many wolves in here. Come on back to my office. Do you two have names?"

"I'm Ilse Schuylkill and this is Wyatt Where. We're associates of Dr. Octavius Bear."

"Oh, so Ernie has called in the big guns, huh!"

"You know Dr. Bear?"

"I know of him. Never met the gentlebeast. Now what do you want to know."

"Were you here when the fight broke out? It was rather late."

"I usually hang around when there's a big game at the Arena. Fights are not uncommon, and we often have to toss a few patrons out. I was here when Ozzie and Joe Jeau started swinging."

"We understood that the argument was actually between Ozzie and the captain of the Orlando Orbiters."

"It started that way but one of the Orbiters gave Ozzie a hard push and knocked him over Joe Jeau. The giraffe was pretty far along in his alcohol consumption. I probably should have cut him off earlier, but he was with a bunch of his buddies, none of whom take too kindly to being deprived. Anyway, Joe Jeau and Ozzie are an explosive mix, especially when they have had a few or more drinks. Head butts, kicks, swinging hoofs. Both teams were trying to break it up. The cops arrived but before they could act, several of the Hombres had pulled Ozzie away. The Orbiters had completely disappeared. What the hell! They had a championship series to play"

"Joe Jeau was totally out of it and was a mess. Ostriches can do a lot of damage. Two of his teammates grabbed him, getting kicked in the process, and I heard them say to the cops that they were going to take him back to his apartment. The whole thing lasted a couple of minutes."

"What happened to Ozzie?"

"He left under his own power with his two Omaha buddies. He didn't seem to be any the worse for wear. Joe Jeau probably got in a few shots, but he was just flailing."

"So as far as you know, with the exception of a bruise and cut or two, Ozzie was OK when he left."

"Yeah, I heard him say he was late for very important appointment."

"Any idea who that might have been?"

"Nope! I doubt he had that many contacts in New York but that's just a guess. Oh, next morning, Ernie Elks offered to pay for any damages. A broken chair and some shattered glassware. Nothing big. Nobody else was hurt except for one of the Hombres who got slugged by a stray foot."

Maury Meerkat

Chapter Eight

Meerkats often are stars on TV.

But they aren't "mere cats," don't you see.

They're mongooses! (mongeese?)

Make this silliness cease.

It's just all too confusing for me.

Back at the hotel, we were waiting in the lounge for the Wolves to return from their interview with Rim Shot management. We compared notes with Belinda, Condo, Otto and Ursula who shared our opinion that a highly motivated outside entity was probably behind the killing. This was no continuation of a bar fight. Octavius mentioned once again that our remit in this case was to demolish any suspicion of guilt on Joe Jeau's part. Period! Ernie was not paying us to solve Ozzie's murder. *(If he was going to pay us, at all!)* If NY law enforcement was ready and willing to drop the charges against the Gotham Giraffe, our job was over.

While we were sitting there we were approached by a pair of ferrets wearing jackets from a local TV network and holding mikes like handheld weapons. A skunk videographer tagged along aiming his camera at the group. Octavius looked at me. One of my more distasteful jobs was dealing with the press.

The female ferret, somewhat taken back by Octavius' size approached the Great Bear and said, "We assume you are Octavius Bear, the famous tycoon and detective."

I intervened. "You assume correctly, but Doctor Bear does not give interviews to the press. I am Maury Meerkat, Doctor Bear's representative. I'll answer your questions, if you have any."

Meanwhile. Octavius and his team all rose and walked off to the elevators, heading up, no doubt, to his suite of rooms. The Wolves had arrived, saw the reporters and our departing group and followed them toward the elevator bank.

The male ferret looked after the now vanishing backs and raced over to intercept Octavius. He managed to get his microphone stuck in the closing doors of the lift. A large pair of paws reopened the doors, and another tossed the mike back over the ferret's head.

I watched this and said, "Your partner doesn't seem to know the meaning of 'No!' does he?"

The female stared at me, recovered her aplomb, and said, "I'm Farrah Ferret, crime reporter for TV Channel 3 here in New York City. My associate *(who was slowly walking back to us)* Fergus Ferret, no relation, covers sports. We understand that Octavius Bear has taken on the case of Joe Jeau Giraffe in the murderous death of Ozzie Ostrich. Is Joe Jeau guilty?

I replied, "We have been requested by Coach Ernie Elks of the Gotham Giraffes to look into the case. He is our client. Coach Elks and Doctor Bear were classmates at Kodiak University. We are assisting NYPD and the team's lawyers in gathering facts and materials concerning the event. I'm sure you know that all of what we uncover is privileged information. We can't comment on Joe Jeau's guilt or innocence. That's what New York pays its district attorneys to do. I'm afraid I have no more I can tell you."

Fergus piped up. "Who have you interviewed and what have you turned up?"

"I guess you have a hearing problem, caused no doubt, by listening to too many cheering crowds. I have no more to tell you."

I gathered up my tail and walked over to the elevators. Fergus and the videographer rushed after me but got caught in a group of teenagers exiting one of the cars. I stepped into the now empty lift, pressed the floor and 'close door' buttons. Time to rejoin my compatriots.

Octavius looked up as I entered the room. "You disposed of the media in your typically diplomatic fashion?"

"More diplomatically than you would have been. Fergus, the sports reporter has been taking 'aggressive' lessons. No doubt we will be on the six o'clock news with lots of commentary and suppositions, but nothing useful from me. What, if anything did you find out at the Rim Shot?"

Wyatt replied, "Not much we didn't already know. Ozzie seemed to be in decent shape when he left the bar. Not so Joe Jeau who was out for the count. Joe Jeau is a regular. Those guys certainly give the lie to giraffes being gentle animals. They've run up huge bills at the bar for replacing furniture, fixtures and glassware. Management has banned a couple of them, including Joe Jeau, in the past. Trouble is, they also spend a lot of money there."

"Speaking of money," I asked, "Could they shed any light on gamblers and gangsters patronizing the place?"

Ilse said, "There were a couple of sharply dressed Dobermans in there talking about the UBA finals. I find it hard to believe they were simply interested in the sport. One of the bartenders identified them as members of a 'sports promotional organization.' She winked when she said it."

"Captain Gorilla probably has more information on them. Ursula, can you shed any light on this?"

"I think I can. As you know, sports gambling is now legal in New York and that has changed the complexion and mix of participants. Estimates are that over 9 billion dollars a year will pass between bettors and casinos and private book makers. While it doesn't dominate the market, basketball is a significant part of the landscape. Open that up to national and international wagering and the number gets stratospheric very rapidly. Nebraska, especially Omaha, has been a gambling mecca for decades although sports betting is partially controlled. Florida has not made it legal but that hasn't constrained many animals. And there's always Las Vegas."

Octavius shrugged. "Well, that certainly leaves us with plenty of candidates."

While we were talking, Chita had strolled in. "God, fashion shows are bizarre. I swear, some of those designers hate females. How goes the great perp search?"

Condo flapped his wings, just missing a floor lamp. "Too many possibles. Our consensus is some gambling syndicate is behind Ozzie's death but that's based on some pretty sketchy data and opinions. Ozzie let several of his Omaha team mates, as well as the Orlando Orbiters, know he was going to file a League grievance against the referees in their semi-final loss. Ursula seems to think he might have had pretty substantial evidence that they were not calling all the fouls on the Orbiters. That grievance could have upset a lot of animals, including gamblers, odds makers, team owners, fans and league officials, to say nothing of the refs themselves."

The Cat looked around. "Has anybody talked to the refs?"

Belinda replied, " 'Dunk' Duncan said he would look into it, but he didn't seem very enthused. Tavi, do you think Captain Gorilla will call them in?"

"I can certainly ask him. We have access to him."

Chita threw up her front paws. "Stupid me! Here I have an interesting tidbit to share and I almost forgot it. The primary reason I go to fashion shows is not to see what horrors the designers have produced this time, although some of their output will still end up in my magazines and websites. The major commodity in play at these events is gossip, the juicier the better."

"One of the runway super-models is an ostrich named Olivia – no surname – just Olivia. With their long legs and neck plus their shaggy powder puff wings, ostriches and emus are favorites of the world's modistes."

"Anyway, it turns out Olivia has a passion for basketball players and has been seen on the wings of several of the Orlando and Omaha team members whenever they are in town. One of those swains turns out to be the unfortunate Ozzie, who I gather had quite a reputation with the ladies. Perhaps, in addition to looking for gamblers and crooked refs, you should 'cherchez la femme' and see what you can dig up. Maybe some jealous mayhem?"

Octavius came out with one of his time-honored 'Hmmms' and said, "Could I interest you in doing a little detecting on the side, Ms. Catt? Perhaps Ursula could give you a paw."

The AI actually giggled and said, "I'd be delighted to work with Chita. It would be different. My work is seldom glamorous or scandalous."

Chita replied, "Somehow, Bear, I thought you'd say that. OK, I'm staying in New York for the rest of the week and I could probably concoct an excuse to interview Olivia for one of my publications. Who knows? It might even be usable. Set me up with a link to Ursula and she can take notes and give me some subtle prompts and after the fact analysis. What do you think, Ursie? Ready for some time on the fast track?"

Ursula laughed. "Ms. Catt, I live on the ultra-fast track. I'll have to slow down a bit."

Chapter Nine

Tigers have an exotic repute.

And their cubs are exceedingly cute.

In a poem or commercial

They're not controversial.

Our two both wear a black and white suit.

The doors to the suite blew open and matching tornados whirled into the room. The twins had returned from their day of adventure. *(I'm sure you missed them.)* Mlle Woof, Ben and Gal took up the rear, obviously exhausted.

"Hi everybody! We're back! When's dinner? Noo Yuck is such a cool place, isn't it, Mlle Woof?"

The Bichon wearily nodded her head and wagged her tail. "Oui, mes petits!"

The Flying Tigers flopped onto an empty couch, clearly done in. "I think the hotel tour guides are going to put in for battle pay." said Gal. "Bearoness and Doctor Bear, you both have a scientific background. If you can figure out a way to harness and channel the energy in those two, you could start a whole new industry."

Octavius laughed. "I guess I could let the pointy heads at UUI take a cut at it. Unfortunately, they're in Kentucky and the twins are usually terrorizing Polar Paradise in the Shetlands. You're also twins. Were you like that when you were kittens?"

"Not really! Our parents were normal tawny tigers. That makes us even more extraordinary. Since we were white, our sire didn't know what to make of us. Our mother, on the other hand, decided to capitalize on our rarity. She paraded us out at shows and posted our pictures on social media. She even arranged for several short films to be made. Ben and I were beginning to feel like we belonged in a freak show. So, we waited until we were about three years old and we ran away and joined the Circus."

Several voices at once. "The Circus?"

Ben laughed. "Don't let Galatea fool you. It was a Flying Circus. No jumping through flaming hoops. Our uncle Felix, a golden tiger, ran a small airport and put on airshows to bring in some extra money. He called them Fearless Felix's Flying Follies. Barnstorming; old bi-planes; even a tri-plane; aerobatics; wing-walking; races; dog-fights; only in our case, it was cat fights. And of course, rides for the audience."

"He never did like our parents. He took us in and started us on odd jobs. Soon, we were learning to fly. One thing led to another. We stuck together and lots of companies were eager to hire a matched team of pilots. Our skills and the classes of airplane we were handling got bigger, faster and more sophisticated. Of course, when you met us, we were flying 747 freighters. But, the thought of piloting the last SST was too good to resist. So, here we are."

I laughed, "Little did you know you would also be trying to corral two wild bear cubs."

"Oh, like everything associated with you folks, they're special and out of the ordinary. We enjoy them and our jobs."

Belinda smiled and said, "And we enjoy having you with us." Looking at Arabella and McTavish, she asked, "Now what mischief did you two get into today?"

"We didn't get into mischief. We did get into the Umpire State Building. It's way tall and we could see all over Noo Yuck. Then we rode the noisy subway down to One Whirled Center. That's even taller but it's closed in. The elevators went 'whoosh.' It's got glass floors on top. That was scary. We were watching the airplanes taking off and landing at Candy Dee, La Gordian and Noo Ark airports. We couldn't see Morristown, so we couldn't check on the Ursa Minor. We ate lunch up there and then took a boat ride out to the Achoo of Libearty. It was a gift from France and it welcomes foreign animals. We couldn't go up to the torch, though."

Mlle Woof interrupted, "While we were on the subway returning here, they wanted to go to Times Square, but we decided it had been a very full day. So, Broadway, Central Park and Grand Central Station are on tomorrow's agenda. Since their mother is in show business and they starred in a Christmas Pantomime at Polar Paradise, *(See Book Eight – The Crank Case)* they want to see a Broadway production. Is that all right?"

Bel laughed and said, "So would I. Let's make a party out of it. Maury, will you call the concierge and see what we can get for tomorrow night? Everyone's invited. We might as well have some fun while we're here."

Octavius looked up, "Speaking of fun, game one of the UBA finals is on tonight. Orlando and Oakland. Do you think we can still get tickets? Bel, can Dunk Duncan do anything?"

"I don't know. I can try. I doubt if we'll have enough seats for everybody, though."

"I'd like to watch those league referees up close and see if Orlando is as good as they say."

Chita yawned. "I'm due for a couturier's cocktail party for the press and influentials tonight. Maybe Olivia will be there or maybe she'll be at the ball game. We'll see. Ursula and I will give you a report if there's anything worth talking about."

Mlle Woof shooed the Cubs out of the room. "Time to wash and change for dinner. You can wear your One World Trade Center T-shirts."

I headed to the concierge desk to see what I could rustle up in the way of a Broadway Show fit for young bears that would also entertain adults. Bel picked up a phone and put through a call to Duncan. Everyone else headed off to get ready for drinks and dinner. Expenses, expenses!

Chita

Chapter Ten

Spotted Cheetah's breathtakingly swift.

It's a really remarkable gift.

From zero to fifty

In no time. How nifty!

And just think! Not one gear must she shift!

The UBA championship series is played at the Jefferson Circle Arena because of its size. It can accommodate 25,000 fans and being in New York has ready access to the media, national and international transportation, accommodations galore and the headquarters of the League. Safety is a top concern, combining Arena, League and NYPD security units. A major but not insurmountable event for the Big Apple.

"Dunk" came through with four courtside seats on the Orlando side of the house. A pair of last minute celebrity no-shows. Octavius took his chair, folded it and pushed it out in the aisle. He sat on the floor. If he didn't, he would have blocked the view of an entire section. But you don't shout "Down in Front" to a nine-foot, 1400-pound bear. Belinda and the two wolves sat next to him. As it was, the surrounding fans were trying to figure out who this humongous ursine was. Some of them recognized the glamorous polar as she stood up, waved, and mouthed "Thank you" to "Dunk" in the VIP box.

(I stayed behind at the hotel, still negotiating seats for 13 folks for a hit Broadway show tomorrow night. This little caper was fast approaching the national debt but hey, if that's the way the Great Bear wanted it, who was I to complain. Anyway, He could probably pay off the national debt.)

Otis and Omar noticed the Wolves, came off the bench and gave them a high five. Coach Oscar was too busy with his lineup and last-minute instructions. Tonight's referees were not the same as at the last semi-final game. The professional leagues use three refs but have been experimenting with four or five. At this game, the number was three, two wildcats and a jaguar, all in striped shirts.

The game got started and Orlando pulled out to an early lead. The Oakland Overlords seemed to be having trouble getting their act together. The Orbiters exhibited some pretty fancy ball handling to the delight of the raucous fans. Otis brought them to their feet with a pair of three-point shots in a row. Omar seemed to own the rebound area. Oakland fought back, and the first quarter ended with Orlando down to a two-point lead. Octavius had brought a lap top with one Ursula aboard. Another copy was out on the town with Chita and God knows how many other manifestations were multitasking about, probably with the Cubs.

The second quarter began and ended much like the first. Rapid fire scoring by both teams. This time Oakland was ahead by five. The refs were calling fouls and to Octavius' unfamiliar eye, things looked like they were on the up-and-up. Half time. Frau Ilse reached into her bag and brought out a keglet of mead for Octavius, a split of champagne for the Bearoness and a bottle of vintage red wine for the Colonel and herself. How she got the bag past security is unknown, but she is capable of high-speed appearances and disappearance.

"Opinions, Ursula?" asked the Great Bear

"My statistical subroutines predict Oakland will take this one by a few points, but Orlando will still win the best of seven series. This championship still has a long way to go. The referees seem to be on the alert and making good calls. Ozzie's threatened complaint may have reached the powers-that-be. I assume you noticed the mass of female "groupies" in the stands going crazy every time Omar scored. The cheerleaders seem to focus on Otis." Right on cue-Oakland won.

As the crowd streamed out of the building and the foursome headed back to the hotel, Colonel Where asked Octavius, "Have you heard any further from Captain Gorilla?"

"No, but I'll check with Maury when we get back. Let's wait and see if Chita comes up with anything from that cocktail party besides a champagne hangover."

*****

Raucous music; clinking drink bowls; plates full of Hors d'Oeuvres; males and females trying to one-up each other with exotic clothing, colored furs and feathers, and tons of bling-bling. A typical couturiers' press party. Chat, Chat, Chat! Laugh, Laugh, Laugh! One or two classic snits. Chita circulated with her laptop at the ready, exposing Ursula's "sensitive sensors" to the madding crowd. Tonight, she appeared as her spotted self, foregoing her frequent black panther outfit. Several press agents and flacks had descended upon her, chatting her up and selling, selling, selling. Then disappearing.

"Chita darling, how lovely to see you. It's been ages. How nice of you to come over from London." The low-pitched growl, punctuated by an occasional howl belonged to a Red Fox named Greta, an avant-garde designer of highly expensive fashionista outfits. "Your publications and websites are taking the industry by storm, even if they're not entirely dedicated to Haute

Couture. You've certainly grown your businesses since taking over from Bearbi Da Savile Row. Is she still in "durance vile?"

"Sadly, yes, Greta, and so is Clarence, her son. Murder and attempted murder go down pretty hard in Old Blighty."

"Well, you seem to have the magic touch even if she didn't. Nice to see you again. I'm on the lookout for Sergio Armadillo. I'm hoping to sell him a new line of female footwear."

"Before you go, Greta. Do you know if Olivia, the Ostrich Supermodel is here tonight? I'm trying to get an interview with her. You know, personality stuff."

"Yes, she is. That's her over there with the bright red feathers and gold choker. I bet she'd kill to have your diamond necklace. She's always in a crowd. Let's see if I can get her attention. I'll introduce you, but she is something of a self-centered, brainless twit. Good luck in getting anything worth printing out of her. C'mon."

As they worked their way through the crowd, Chita whispered, "OK Ursula. Ready to do your stuff?"

"Roger, Ms. Catt."

Greta let out a discreet howl and Olivia turned from her clutch of admirers to direct a glassy stare at the fox. "Oh, hello Gracie. Nice to see you!"

"It's Greta, dear. I designed some of the outfits you've been wearing at the show."

"Oh, of course. Silly Me!"

"Olivia, I want to introduce you to Madame Catherine Catt, better known as Chita. Madame Catt runs an empire of publications and websites dedicated to females from her headquarters in London. She is interested in interviewing you for one or more of her magazines and websites. You know, life and times of a supermodel. Chita, meet Olivia. Olivia, meet Chita and now excuse me while I search down my patrone."

The idea of being in international print registered in Olivia's slightly drink-sodden brain and she turned from her admirers and gave Chita what is the 'struthio camelus' equivalent of a winsome smile. "You'd like to interview me?"

"Yes, I'm sure that's no novelty for someone as famous as you are but my audiences are worldwide, and a little more publicity of the right kind certainly can't hurt."

"I suppose so. I'd so much like to hit it bigger in Europe and the Mid-East. American modeling is so constraining. Would you like to talk now? Sorry, my agent isn't here tonight."

"Well, I'm heading back to England in the morning and I'd really like to get your story tonight. I have a voice activated laptop we can use to take down the interview. I'll send any of the material we intend to publish to your agent for approval and in turn, we'd like some publicity photos of you."

"I guess that'd be all right, then. Let's go to a quiet corner, if we can find one." She giggled.

"There's a bar on the lower floor. Maybe we can go there."

Down to the bar, several drinks ordered, Chita brought out the Ursula-bearing laptop, did the introductory identification blurbs and started off. "We already have your biography and lists of shows you've been in and will be in, so we don't have to spend time going over those. What I want to do is share with my readers and watchers what it's like to be a supermodel day by day. What do you do for fun? How do you spend your time off the runway? Are you into sports? Where do you live? With whom? Any boyfriends you want to mention? What's next for you?"

Olivia sighed, "Where to begin? I just moved into my own apartment on the East Side. I had been sharing with another model, but we had a falling out. Between photo shoots, fashion shows and TV appearances, I've been very busy. But they're getting pretty stale. I want some new excitement. I'd like more travel to exotic places – first class of course. Have you ever been to Africa? I think my family came from there. My egg hatched here in America in a bird sanctuary. Even when I was little, I knew I was exceptional. My legs and neck are just the right proportions and my feathers are so luxurious that I occasionally have to cut them back. I was made for modelling."

Chita grinned, "Yes, I've been to Africa. I was born there. Let's talk about your interests. Are you into sports?"

"Oh yes. I love badminton. Play it every chance I get, and I run to keep my figure in shape. But my real passion is basketball. I'm wild about it. In fact, if I didn't have a contract to be here tonight, I would be over at Jefferson Arena watching the first game of the finals. I just love the Orlando Orbiters and the Omaha Hombres. I don't care that much for Oakland."

"Anyone special on those teams?"

"Well, I did have a thing going with Ozzie from the Hombres but he's dead now."

"I heard that. They say it was murder. I'm very sorry!"

"Oh, don't be. He was beginning to be a bore. Pushy and much too demanding, if you know what I mean. We wouldn't have lasted. My current squeeze is Omar on the Orbiters. He's so much more sophisticated. He's very smooth and really talented. He's going to move in with me during the off season. I'm going to see him after tonight's game, so I'll have to cut this short. I'll have my agent send you a set of fact sheets and a package of photos. I just had new ones made with updated clothes from the latest shows. I just love your diamond necklace. Where can I get one like that? I'll tell Omar."

"This is a one-of-a-kind I had made in Paris. I paid extra to make it an exclusive. Sorry!"

"Oh, that's all right. I'm more of a ruby and sapphire girl myself. Well, ta-ta, I'll be looking forward to seeing myself in your publications." She strutted off, a bit stiffly. Champagne at work?

Chita chuckled "Well, Ursula, what do you think?"

"What a bimbo!! That certainly puts Omar in the crosshairs, doesn't it? A jealous rage and disposal of a rival? Make it look like a follow-up fight with Joe Jeau or a run-in with the gambling syndicate. This is getting more complex by the minute. We need to play this back for Dr. Bear."

Chapter Eleven

Mamselle Woof minds the Cubs while they play.
She corrects and protects them each day.
But addressing her, please,
Do not say Bichon Freeze.
Her name's French and it's Bichon Freezay!

Back at the suite, Octavius, Belinda, the Wolves and I sat listening to Ursula's playback of the interview. Chita was toying with a bowl of champagne.

I snorted, "Sentimental sort, isn't she?"

The cat laughed, "Fortunately, she's stupid, too. Have I been to Africa? Jeez!"

Belinda, her theatrical background showing, said, "There's a million of them. All legs and neck and no brain. But she's certainly opened up another dimension to this case. Do you really think Omar might have killed Ozzie to get him out of the way?"

Octavius grunted. "It could have been one of those 'I've got your girl now, so get lost.' conversations that turned into a brawl. Remember, these guys are pretty quick to exert muscle. She thinks Omar is smooth and sophisticated. What I saw out there tonight on the arena floor was rough and tumble raised to the nth degree. We'll have to bring this to Captain Gorilla's attention although we are a bit short in the proof department. Our other scenarios still hold water."

Colonel Where looked up and said, "They're not mutually exclusive. The gambling syndicates may still be a powerful factor in this situation. Joe Jeau is looking less and less likely as our murderer, however. But, as you say, we could use a little more proof. Any ideas, Ursula?"

The AGI responded, "I think it's time to revisit the police. They may not think much of the jealousy angle. I think Captain Gorilla still thinks Joe Jeau is guilty. But another basketball player could be a likely candidate. By the way, Chita. That was a most interesting experience. But a little goes a long way. Doctor Bear, I'm glad you're not into couture. I will make you a video recording of the interview to take to the police."

"Thanks Ursula! You're not going back to London tomorrow, are you, Chita?"

The cat shook her head, "I just said that to get her to talk to me tonight."

"Maury, what have Condo and Otto been up to?"

"I think they're following up on the gamblers and the referees."

"OK, let's all get together first thing tomorrow and compare notes.

Belinda asked, "Were you able to get show tickets for all of us?"

"Yep, 13 tickets to The Lion King."

*****

Breakfast! Once again, we dominated the J.W. Marmoset dining room. Once again, the Cubs were having a rollicking time tossing muffins back and forth. Once again, Mlle Woof was frantically trying to calm them down. Today, they were going to Central Park, the United Nations, and Grand Central Station with intermittent rides on the subway. They both wanted to ride in the front of the first car and look at the tracks and the signals as the train shot from station to station. Juvenile energy was at a peak. Tonight, they would go to Broadway and Times Square, gape at the lights and then join the rest of us at the Minskoff Theater for the musical.

The Flying Tigers joined the adults at our large table. A little relief from smaller persons. I mentally called the roll. Thirteen animals present and accounted for. After the business of ordering food and drink was taken care of, Octavius, who was seated on a couch requisitioned from the lobby, looked around and noisily cleared his throat.

"OK, let's bring each other up to speed. Belinda, Frau Ilse, Colonel Where and I went to the ball game. Oakland won but not by much. The refs seemed to be doing their job well. A little unnecessary roughness but nothing out of the ordinary that I could see. 25,000 screaming fans. Did I miss anything important, Ursula?"

The AGI unit replied from a large laptop sitting in the middle of the table. The dining room wait staff was used to meetings with remote hookups and didn't blink an eye at the talking computer. Little did they know who was doing the talking.

"No, Doctor Bear, although in view of our next discussion, I should note that Omar and Otis on the Orbiters were getting more than their fair share of attention from the groupies and cheerleaders. Those two are consummate showboats."

Chita segued in with her brief report of the fashion cocktail party and then let Ursula play back the interview with Olivia. Raised eyebrows *(by those who had them)* all around the table. Condo and Otto, who were hearing this for the first time, jumped to the same conclusion we had reached the night before. Add one more motive and possible perpetrator to the list.

Ben asked, "Have they found the weapon yet?"

I replied, "Not that we know of. We need to check in with Captain Gorilla after we finish here. Condo, Otto any luck on the gambling front?"

"We've made some progress, thanks a great deal to our Ursula. It won't be any news to you that a lot of money is riding on these games. What is interesting is the number of bet variations there are. Point spreads, over and under total points, individual scoring, individual fouls, believe it or not, and all kinds of propositions ranging from number of rebounds, successful free throws, even how much time a player spends on the court or on the bench. If you want to lose money on basketball there are almost an infinite number of ways to do it and a very substantial number of bookies who are willing to take your action. We've been concentrating on the Big Kahunas. The kind that would consider murder just another enforcement tool. Even then, the number is big but not unmanageable."

Galatea snorted. "I didn't understand a word you just said. I guess we Flying Tigers gamble our lives, not our money."

Condo laughed, "I fly too, you know. My knowledge of gambling is lately come by courtesy of Ursula. Ursie, any comments?"

"A suggestion. We ought to talk with Joe Jeau and Ernie again. Without accusing them of anything, we can probably get the names of the most likely 'Big Kahunas' from them. There isn't a player or coach alive who hasn't been approached. Make sure their lawyers are there."

Otto squeaked, "Good idea. What do you think, Octavius?"

"I agree, but let me call Ernie first and line it up. Then you two plus Ursula can go on a fact-finding mission. Maury, you, Wyatt and I need to catch up with Captain Gorilla. Ben and Gal, I assume you're going to be with the little terrors again today along with Mlle Woof."

They looked at each other and then over at the table where the twins were sitting, shrugged and said. "I guess we get to go tourist again."

"Let's see if we can get any more insight into this Olivia-Omar thing. Bel, Frau Ilse and Chita. Can you ladies check out the Fashion Week show today and see if you can stir up any more gossip?"

Chita and Bel nodded. The Frau said, "Ach, I hate those things but all right."

"Does each team have an Ursula?"

Affirmative. Ursula's multi-tasking was becoming more and more essential.

"OK, let's finish breakfast and get on with it. I'll call Ernie."

Condo and Otto sat down with Ursula and strategized their approach while Octavius made the call.

"Ursie," asked the Otter, "who are some of the most likely big-time gamblers who take a serious interest in basketball?"

"One name sticks out, Otto. 'Paulie the Puma' heads up a syndicate of bookies and enforcers who will take your action in the States and overseas. There are over 7000 pro basketball players in Europe, Asia, Australia and the Middle East alone plus some in South America. It's a big business and Paulie has his paw in just about every area."

Condo gulped. "He's not related to Pontius Puma, is he? He's the Brazilian hoodlum whose network I destroyed and who got arrested after trying to burn down Octavius' mansion and UUI."

"No relation to Paulie. Pontius is still in prison here in the States. Brazil doesn't have an extradition treaty with the U.S., so he's stuck in our federal prison for selling military technology illegally and attempted murder for the fire storms he tried on the Bear's Lair and UUI. Chita was mated to him, but no longer. *(See Book Three -The Case of the Spotted Band.)*

"Yeah, we know about Chita. I guess Pumas are generally nasty. It runs with the species."

Octavius returned. "Ernie will have Joe Jeau and his two lawyers in his office in an hour."

Otto asked, "Does he know what we want to talk to him about?"

"I told him we were following several leads and we could use his and Joe Jeau's advice."

"Are you, Wyatt and Maury going to see Captain Gorilla?"

"Yes. We'll have a copy of Ursula with us, too. She can tell us what you find out from Ernie, Joe Jeau and the lawyers. Instant cross communication."

"And the ladies are off to the Fashion Shows."

"Chita, Belinda, Frau Ilse and Ursula."

"Ursula certainly gets around. Lucky for us."

"She'll also be with the Cubs as they once again invade Noo Yuck."

91

I looked at Octavius. "Have you ever figured out how many simultaneous instances she is capable of supporting without slowing down or blowing something?"

"We did a test run once, Maury. We shut her down at 125. No problem with her. Our test instruments couldn't keep up. She claims the number is infinite. She may be right."

"How do the techies at UUI do maintenance on her?"

"They don't do much. She is becoming increasingly self-maintaining."

"So, she's going autonomous?"

"Or a reasonable facsimile thereof."

"Oh, boy!"

Chapter Twelve

Condors fly through the Andean air.

In the States they're incredibly rare.

They can endlessly soar

On wings ten feet or more.

Climbing high in the sky with no care.

Otto, Condo and Ursula arrived at Ernie's office to find Jerry Basen and Joni Cockatoo engaged in intense discussion with the coach. No Joe Jeau!

Ernie looked up as they entered. "Good morning, Gentlebeasts! We'll be with you in just a moment. Joe Jeau had to check in with NYPD and is on his way here. He's wearing an ankle monitor that's annoying him no end."

Joni asked, "Where's your boss?"

Condo answered *(black bird to black bird)* "He's off following another lead. We're here to ask you and your client a few questions that will help us narrow this situation down."

Just as he finished speaking, the door opened, and Joe Jeau loped in, ducking his head as he came. "Hey, when are we going to wrap this mess up? I'm sick of the cops and this ankle monitor is the worst."

Otto stared upward at the Giraffe and said, "We need some advice and information from you. We want to talk about gambling and gamblers. Counselors, before you come unglued, this whole conversation is strictly confidential, and we are not accusing anyone of anything. *(He didn't mention the silent Ursula in his backpack.)* As you know, Ozzie claimed he was going

93

to file a grievance with the League about what he called "crooked refereeing." That could only mean one thing. Somebody stood to make a lot of money if Omaha lost. We think Pauli the Puma or several of his 'employees' may be involved and we need help in tracking them down. I can't imagine that both Ernie and you don't get approached over and over during the course of a season. What can you tell us that will give us a lead? Are some of the refs 'crooked' like Ozzie claimed? Who should we be going after? None of you will identified as sources."

Both Joe Jeau and Ernie looked at the lawyers. Ernie said, "I trust these guys and I'm their client. All right, what do you want to know?"

"Let's start with the refs."

Joe Jeau snorted. "If you want to know anything about 'crooked' refs, you have to start with the League office. If there's a fix going to be put in, that's where it will start."

"You mean 'Dunk' Duncan?"

Ernie said, "Maybe not 'Dunk' himself but that Kangaroo has some strange characters 'working' for him."

"More please!"

"So-called League officials who seem to have no job description and can be found at the games but do nothing."

"Got any names?"

"Smith, Jones, Brown…none you can believe."

"Are they hanging around the finals games? Could you identify any of them?"

"Not without taking some heat. I don't want to end up like Ozzie."

"You think they may have offed Ozzie?"

"Can't prove it, but I wouldn't be surprised."

At this point, Joni Cockatoo interrupted. "I think that's more than enough, Gentlebeasts. My client is not going to involve himself in any more jeopardy than he already has."

"Well, I guess we'll have to pay 'Dunk' a visit. We'll just tell him we're following up on Ozzie's threat to file a grievance and see where that takes us. I hope we'll be able to get that ankle monitor off you in the next few days, Joe Jeau."

"Can't be too soon, Dude. Thanks."

Otto asked, "Do either of you lawyers have any thoughts you want to share before we go?"

Jerry Basen yodeled and then said, "That's what we were discussing when you arrived. Ozzie didn't have many friends. He seemed to have a talent for 'bad-mouthing.' I'm wondering if it wasn't a falling out about money, professional rivalry, female problems or maybe just a stupid argument that got out of control."

Joni joined in. "Often, the worst crimes are committed for the dumbest of reasons. I could give you a list as long as your wing, Senhor Condor."

"Point taken, Ms. Cockatoo. Mr. Basen, we are pursuing several of those possibilities. Please remember. We have been assigned to prove that Joe Jeau didn't kill Ozzie. That may or may not involve determining who the real culprit is. By the way, Joe Jeau, did the police determine what your blood alcohol level was when they arrested you? You may have been incapable of beating Ozzie up."

Joni Cockatoo chortled, "That's our primary defense. Senhor Condor. It was four times normal. A lesser animal might be dead. Joe Jeau was completely out of it and the police know it. He couldn't have even gotten to the crime scene."

"We'll follow up on that. Thanks for your time. We'll be back, Ernie."

As they exited the building, Condo spoke to the AGI. "Did you get all that, Ursula?

"Yes, I did. Interesting about Joe Jeau's alcohol level. I'll pass all of it on to Doctor Bear before he goes to see Captain Gorilla. Ozzie is turning out to be a fight looking to happen. I am also with Chita, the Frau and the Bearoness. I wonder if we'll be able to pick up any more about the Olivia triangle. My probability algorithms keep shifting back and forth on the most likely killer candidates.

We also need to discuss how to face down 'Dunk" Duncan and his non-performing staff. Who are these guys? I'll do a search on all known associates of Pauli the Puma. We'll then have to identify them as being at the finals. It seems likely that Ozzie was right, and the fix was, and probably still is, in with the referees. Fascinating."

*****

NYPD headquarters! Captain Gorilla had agreed to see Octavius, Wyatt and me and compare notes.

"Good morning, Gentlebeasts. I suppose Joe Jeau is chafing at the bit or whatever Giraffes do, to get that cuff off."

"Good morning, Captain. He wants more than that. He wants to be cleared and I don't blame him. I was recently under suspicion for murder and it's not very comfortable." *(See Book Seven -The Suit Case)*

"You, Doctor Bear? I'm amazed."

"So was I. I'll tell you the story sometime. Obviously, I was cleared. By the way, can we make this a first name relationship? I'm Octavius and my two companions are Wyatt Where and Maury Meerkat. Wyatt and Maury." *(No mention of Ursula.)*

"Sure. Call me Gordon when I'm not with any of my staff."

"OK, Gordon. Do you want go first?"

"Well, we're not much further along than we were when we last talked. We still haven't found the weapon and we have a very distinct shortage of witnesses – like none. I'll grant you that what we have on Joe Jeau is mostly circumstantial and hearsay. The DA doesn't think he can get an indictment on what we have. We'll probably reduce him to a person of interest and take off the monitor."

"Did you check the alcohol level in his blood stream when you arrested him in his apartment?"

"Yeah, that's one of the reasons we're downgrading his status. He had enough liquor in him to stop a <u>herd</u> of Giraffes. He was completely out of it and his teammates who took him home confirm it. I doubt he could have found the crime scene, much less given Ozzie a fatal fight."

97

"That's what we and his lawyers think, too. Any other ideas?"

"Nah, it's your turn."

"Well, there's a couple of threads we're following. First, we've reviewed the video of the game and Ozzie was right. Especially in the fourth quarter, the referees were missing a number of fouls by Orlando. It also turns out there are a few suspicious characters on the League office payroll who seem to do nothing. We're trying to track them back to Paulie the Puma or some other big-time gamblers. We have one theory that when Ozzie threatened to file a grievance, someone thought it was time to shut him up. There's two parts to this. One: Is the League office and 'Dunk' Duncan playing footsies with the Big Kahunas? If so, that's probably a case for the FBI. Two: Are one or more of those League hangers-on really gang enforcers? We have some reason to believe so, but we can't prove it. That part seems like a job for NYPD."

"Thanks!"

"Don't mention it. There's one other item. It seems Ozzie was having an affair with the Supermodel Olivia. You know, the one whose legs go on forever and whose neck can handle a ton of jewelry. Seems Olivia had gotten bored with Ozzie *(too pushy)* and had turned her significant attentions to Omar on the Orlando Orbiters. He's moving in with her in the offseason. That opens up a theory of jealous suitors having it out."

"Where did you get all this?"

"From the lady herself. One of our team members is the publisher of several major female's magazines and social media sites. *(Given her shady past, Octavius failed to identify Chita by name.)* This is Fashion Week in

New York and she caught up with Olivia and got a short interview with her. She volunteered her personal situation. Supermodel beautiful but also super dumb. Of course, she didn't say anything about Omar and Ozzie going at each other but with her self-centered ego, she'd probably just think it was her due. We have a team of ladies at today's fashion show. Gossip galore! If they turn anything more up on the Olivia thing, we'll let you know."

The Gorilla frowned. "I assume Omar is still in town. The championship hasn't been played out. Think I'll have a chat with old Omar. He might end up thinking twice about moving in with Miss Legs. Any other thoughts? Maury, Wyatt?"

The Wolf looked over. "Just one. Ozzie was a Class-A put down artist. He made lots of enemies on his own team and others. I realize it makes your job tougher but the number of animals who would rejoice at his demise is probably quite large."

"You're right. That doesn't help much at all.

I piped up. "It probably wouldn't have helped his grievance submission much either. He was a known griper. But even so, I'm sure the League, the refs and the big money gamblers could have done without the hassle."

Octavius had the last word. "If you are going to drop the charges against Joe Jeau, that actually finishes up my obligation to Ernie Elks. I'll have to talk with the Coach."

"How about hanging around a few more days and giving the NYPD a little more support."

"Well, my Cubs are having a love affair with 'Noo Yuck' and Belinda is crazy about the city, so maybe we can stretch it a bit. We are all descending on the Lion King show tonight. That should be interesting. As for today, I'll let you know what we hear from the Fashionistas, if anything."

The Gorilla smiled. "We've stopped recording."

When we got outside, I chuckled. "Maybe he stopped recording, but we didn't. Got everything, Ursula?"

"Yes, Maury. I guess the only real news we got from him was the charges against Joe Jeau being dropped. I'd love to hear his conversation with Omar."

"If you can pull that off, I don't want to know how you did it."

The AGI giggled.

"Any news yet from the fashion show?"

"They've only just arrived. If Chita runs into Olivia again, she'll have to explain why she didn't go back to London this morning."

"Don't worry about Chita," growled the Bear. She has a long history of made-up stories. Let's get back to the hotel. I want to call Ernie and the lawyers. They can break the news to Joe Jeau. I also want to make contact with the FBI to get them going on the League office."

Chapter Thirteen

Fashion shows boast "creations" galore,

But the Frau thinks they're really a bore.

Olivia's back,

Dressed in silver and black,

And she limps as she moves down the floor.

At the New York Fashion Show in Bryant Park. Chita had used her press credentials to get front row seats for Alfonso Aardvark's runway extravaganza. She looked at Belinda and Frau Ilse and said, "Alfonso is famous for his off-the-wall creations. I don't know who buys them. Do you know, Ursula?"

The Artificial Intelligence Unit, unwilling to speak in the close surroundings, flashed a series of names on the screen of the laptop that Belinda was carrying. "Wow," said the Bearoness, "that's quite a who's who. I guess they have more money than sense."

The Frau gave out a growl-snort that sounded like a sneeze. "What a waste! Females being brow beaten into ridiculous costumes for the sake of keeping up. Give it to charity, instead. Chita, your publications encourage this nonsense!"

The Cat smiled and replied, "Just remember the number of animals who are employed by these fashion houses, including uneducated females who make some of the fabrics and trim that go into these 'creations.' The fashion industry, silly though it may seem, keeps a lot of individuals from starvation. I agree that some of these designs are ridiculous and ridiculously-priced, but clothing is still a powerful economic force."

Before the discussion could go any further, the lights lowered, a drum roll crashed, and a cloying female voice welcomed the audience to sit back and enjoy the latest Alfonso's conceptions. Unfortunately, she went on describing each creation and the profound message behind it.

The models began their struts down the catwalk to the dramatic strum of several guitars. Follow spots highlighted their slinks and shakes. First: a sleek greyhound sporting a long flowing cape that spread out behind like a bridal veil. Long dangling earrings and a jaunty cap. Behind her came a palomino in western garb. A leopard wearing a transparent gold jumpsuit that accented her spots.

In the number four position, Olivia approached. The narrator said something unintelligible about outer space. On her tiny head she wore a band that sprouted antennae in all directions. Her gigantic eyes were accented with thick black lashes. Her extra-long neck was covered with fine spun reflective silver gauze. Her body and wings were striped in black and silver and on her fabulous legs she wore silver shorts. Her strut was very stiff, almost a limp. No doubt blinded by the follow spots and the flashing lights from cameras, she didn't seem to notice Chita sitting in the front row. "Just as well," thought the Cat, "no need for excuses as to why I didn't go back to London, if she even remembered."

And so it went for the better part of forty minutes. Design after design. Model after model from a delicious selection of species. Then came an intermission to allow slurping of mid-morning champagne, chatting and gossip and resetting of the stage, catwalk and of course, the models.

"You were a runway model in Paris, weren't you Chita?"

"Right, Bearoness, only I usually appeared as a slinky black panther. At the time, I wasn't too keen on showing my real identity. Oh wait, there's someone I want to talk with. Greta, Greta darling. Hello again."

The designing Red Fox trotted over, balancing a champagne bowl and several Hors d'Oeuvres in her paws. She said hello with her mouth full and practically choked. Laughter all around.

"Greta, I want you to meet two absolutely fabulous ladies. *(Ursula was not to be mentioned.)* First, this is the famous aquastar, very wealthy member of Scottish aristocracy and wife of the equally famous Octavius Bear. Meet Bearoness Belinda Béarnaise Bruin Bear (nee Black)."

"Oh," gushed Greta, "What a pleasure. I have wanted to meet you for so long. You are even lovelier than the media make you out to be. What brings you to New York and Fashion Week?"

"Chita and I are partners in a couple of business ventures and she persuaded me to make the trip. To say it's been interesting is a major understatement. But let me introduce a most wonderful companion of mine, Frau Ilse Schuylkill-Where. Ilse has been an associate of Octavius for many years and she has also worked with me on many projects. You would be hard pressed to find a more beautiful, clever, talented and I probably shouldn't say, dangerous she-wolf. Among other things she is, as am I, a highly skilled pilot and she has several of the highest military honors to her credit."

The Red Fox stared at the Frau in wonderment. "Hello Frau Ilse. Aren't you a beauty. Ever thought of modelling?" The Frau shook her head vehemently. Not for her!

"You have some amazing friends, Chita. But tell me, how did your interview with Olivia go last night?"

"It was short, but I found out several things I hadn't known. She has this thing for basketball centers. First Ozzie on the Omaha Hombres and now Omar with Orlando. He's moving in with her. She didn't seem at all upset about Ozzie's death. Last night, she seemed to be moving stiffly. I thought she had too much to drink but I noticed she was the same on the runway today. Does she always move like that?"

"Well, of course, all catwalk models strut. You should know that, but now that you mention it, she does seem to be almost limping. I hadn't really noticed but let's see how she does in the finale. Alfonso isn't one of my favorites, but he does know how to put on a spectacle."

Greta was right. The finale was spectacular. Even the Frau was impressed. A laser show coupled with other high-speed lights and strobes set off the runway. Wild music with a thumping beat as the models streamed down the catwalk to wild applause. Olivia was moving very stiffly.

When it was over, Belinda turned to Greta and said, "It was lovely meeting you, Greta. Do you put on shows?"

The Fox replied, "Yes, but most of my income is from designs I sell to other couturiers. I actually couldn't afford to put on one of these Fashion Week extravaganzas. Small intimate events are more my style."

The Bearoness looked at the Frau and Chita and said, "I'd better get back to my offspring. They're probably back from their morning adventures and starving to death."

It was a short cab ride from Bryant Park back to the hotel and sure enough, Arabella and McTavish were there, telling anyone who would listen how hungry they were. They had gone to Grand Central Station. "It's really big and we saw all the trains on the platforms and all the animals rushing to get off or on."

Then a few blocks east to the UN where the flags of all the countries flapped in the breeze. McTavish was more interested in the East River, the barges and the bridges. Arabella bought a book with world maps, flags and descriptions of the member countries. She was searching in vain for Scotland until one of the Flying Tigers pointed out that Scotland was part of the United Kingdom. She then repeatedly announced this fact to all and sundry and proudly displayed the map of the UK and the Scottish flag.

This afternoon, Central Park and maybe one of the 'moozyums.' But tonight was the big treat. They were going to see the Lion King with real lions. Of course, they knew Lion from the Lion and Unicorn pub back home, but he wasn't a King. Off they went with Mlle Woof's normally jaunty tail at half mast and the Flying Tigers moving at well below flight speed.

Chapter Fourteen

Honey Badger is fierce as can be.

She's an FBI agent, you see.

She can get awfully rough,

On a gangster or tough.

I don't think I'd like her chasing me.

Octavius placed a call to Ernie Elks only to find that Captain Gorilla had beaten him to the punch and had informed Joni Cockatoo that Joe Jeau was now regarded as a "Person of Interest" rather than a "Suspect." He told her to bring him in to 1PP to have the ankle monitor removed. They had gone off like the proverbial shot.

The Great Bear stayed on the line with Ernie and Jerry Basen to further explore the gambling and crooked refs angle. I listened in. Ursula was operating in silent mode. "There's another game tonight. So far, the officiating seemed honest enough in Game One but that was a different set of referees from the semi-final that Ozzie was complaining about."

"Yeah, we're familiar with the Game One crew. No problems that we know of. I don't know who's on tonight. As I think you know, the big money is on the final championship outcome, but there's plenty of cash riding each night on the game itself, the point spread, over and under and bunch of other bets. You know, we've been concentrating on the officials, but you can't rule out the players and coaches, either."

"Do you suspect anyone?"

"Not on the Oakland team. I'm not that familiar with them. We never play them, but that Omar on the Orbiters sets my nose to twitching."

"How so?"

"Now, most of these players make damn good money and some of them have a fast-lane life style. But Omar is in the supersonic-lane. Literally. He rents an executive jet; eats and drinks at the fanciest restaurants; drives high-end, customized sports cars; constantly has one or more classy females on his wing and keeps plush apartments in several major cities. Maybe he can afford it, but he may be supplementing his income somehow."

"Has anyone followed up on these suspicions?"

"The League has an ethics office, but I've never heard of them investigating Omar."

"I happen to know that he is about to move in with the Supermodel Olivia. She used to date Ozzie."

"How did you come by that piece of information?"

"Sources, Ernie, sources. That's what keeps us private investigators ahead of the game."

"Well, I guess you filled your part of our bargain, Octavius. Joe Jeau's not entirely in the clear but I can't ask you to hang around until they drop the 'Person of Interest' tag. If that heats up, I may call on you again."

"I'm planning on staying in New York for a few more days. My Cubs love the place and you owe them a basketball game."

"So I do. Bring them around tomorrow morning and I'll get a couple of the guys to do a little one-on-one with them. That way they can say they played against the championship Gotham Giraffes."

"They'll go crazy. We're all going to see the Lion King tonight. The two of them are stage-struck after being in a Christmas pantomime we put on at the castle in the Shetlands. *(See Book Eight – The Crank Case)* Unfortunately, we'll miss Game Two."

"I'll tell you about it in the morning. So long, Octavius. Thanks again."

"De nada!"

After he hung up, the Bear pulled up Ursula and looked at me. "Well, you two. What do you think?"

The hyper-speed AGI responded first. "I've already started a search on Omar. He does lead a very luxurious life style which of itself is not a crime but worth exploring. I have the name of tonight's officials. I'm doing a background check as we speak."

As soon as Ms. Smarty-Circuit shut up, I added, "I think we need to talk to the FBI. I'll give Agent Honey Badger a call. *(See Book Seven - The Suit Case)*

"Good idea. I doubt if she can handle this herself from Detroit, but she can put you on to the best agents to deal with our suspicions. I'm sure the Bureau is probably on it already."

He was right. Special Agent Honey Badger is a good friend and law enforcement supporter that I have come to enjoy working with. When I called her, she was out on a case but got back to me in relatively short order.

"Hey, Meerkat, que pasa? Got something for me or is this just a social call?"

"Hi, Honey, how are you doing?"

"Oh, you know, still trying for a transfer to Chicago but Detroit keeps me busy enough. What's up?"

"I need a referral. We've been working in New York on a murder case. Maybe you've heard about it. An Omaha Hombre basketball player named Ozzie Ostrich was found dead in an alley near the Jefferson Circle Arena. This was after he had an earlier bar fight with a member of the Gotham Giraffes, Joe Jeau Giraffe. Joe Jeau was arrested for the murder. We were called in by the Gotham Giraffes' manager Ernie Elks, an old pal of Octavius, to investigate and hopefully get Joe Jeau exonerated. It turns out that Joe Jeau had passed out in his apartment after the fight and was so drunk he couldn't possibly have gotten up, found or killed the ostrich."

"That's all background. We still don't know who killed Ozzie, but he was about to file a grievance complaint against the referees who officiated at the semi-final championship game that the Hombres lost to the Orlando Orbiters. We have a strong suspicion that gamblers were involved and may have offed Ozzie to shut him up. Can you put me in touch with the agent responsible for monitoring sports gambling? Octavius and I want to compare notes and information."

"Sure! That would be Bill Bison, Assistant Director of the Criminal Investigative Division. They have a Task Force dedicated to gambling violations and work with the Internal Revenue Service in tracking down illegal actors and activities. Give me your cell phone number and I'll have him call you. Does Octavius know him?"

109

"Probably. Let me give you both of our numbers. Thanks, Honey. I suppose you heard the final story on the death of the Musk Ox. It turned out to be a wild and wooly affair involving a very hostile alternate universe. Birds! Seems we're always dealing with birds. "

"Yeah, I got a report after that attempted gassing of the MIT professor in Cambridge."

"Well, if you have any doubts on whether alternative universes exist, put them to bed. We have significant proof that they do. Our team is hard at work exploring, defining and refining." *(See Book Seven – The Suit Case)*

"Hey, after we get you going on this sports gambling case, you'll have to give me a more detailed briefing on these different worlds. I guess the government has some clandestine agencies working on this that I don't know about."

"Oh yeah, try General Turmoil and his non-existent group called The Business. They're a scary bunch, especially him. We've crossed paths and swords with him a number of times. He'd like nothing better than to have Octavius bow out of this arena. Ain't gonna happen! Thanks for the referral. I'll be back."

I reported back to the Great Bear. He knew Bill Bison but not very well. He said he'd wait for the Assistant Director's call. Meanwhile, Ursula had done a scan on tonight's referees. Believe it or not, they were all zebras. They wore their own stripes. Nothing seriously awry to report. Among the three of them, they had 22 years in the officiating business. A couple of complaints lodged but they were the usual close judgement calls that some players or coaches didn't like. No consistent patterns.

She also had unearthed some interesting facts about Omar's finances and lifestyle. He's been playing with the pros for eight years after playing college ball in Africa. His family is reasonably well off but hardly rich. He went to college on several sports scholarships. He was drafted by the Orbiters and given a substantial signing bonus within the League's limits. By his third year, he was consistently playing in the starting five and that's when his taste for expensive luxuries blossomed. He has an $18 million-dollar annual contract with Orlando and a lot of endorsements. The guess is he pulls down between $40 and 50 million a year. He also sends money back to his large family in Africa. That's all Ursula could make out from his tax records, bank accounts and publicly available contracts. You could make a marginal case that he is overspending and that his income is being supplemented by off-the-record sources, but more evidence is needed.

We put our theory in the suspense category.

*****

The AGI rang her chime. "Excuse me! I need to speak with Doctor Bear. Howard has updated the status of their research on electrons coming in from Biosphere Z. There definitely is a sentient presence there. The pattern of transmissions is too orderly to be simple random bursts. They may not be aware that Howard and Marlin are on the other end. I'm sure they know they're sending to someone, but they may not know who."

As part of Project Multiverse, an Octavius sponsored program, Howard the Porcupine Genius and Marlin the Dolphin, his partner, have been expanding on the quantum phenomenon of electrons coupling over long distances. Earlier experiments in electron entanglement have resulted in "quantum teleportation" over relatively short distances. They are seeking to

111

apply the principle to alternate universes whose distances are not readily measured. As shown in previous volumes of the Casebooks of Octavius Bear, there is ample proof that alternate universes do exist and, in some cases, thrive with sentient and non-sentient life. We have had adventures in traveling to some of these locations and have also been visited by several of their denizens.

Unfortunately, not all these encounters have been friendly. Most have not. Add to that the conflicts we have had with the aforementioned General Turmoil and you can understand that Multiverse hunting can be a dangerous job.

I will be passing all of this and more to Agent Badger next time I talk to her

Chapter Fifteen

Is he mountain lion, cougar or puma(r)?

Is he nasty or is that a rumor?

Paulie has this distinction.

He is facing extinction.

That can impact a cat's sense of humor.

The call from Assistant Director Bison came through on Octavius' phone. We were told to expect a call shortly from Special Agent Malcolm Malamute in the New York office. Malamute was heading up a team that was looking into a series of suspicious activities surrounding the UBA and especially the current championship series. Our ears perked up over that. If the Bureau had suspicions, that added some weight to our investigations. We needed to merge and meld.

Ursula had managed to bring up the UBA's human resources roster. "There were four animals on the payroll with amorphous titles like: Assistant Infrastructures Manager; League Logistics Supervisor; Uniform Design Associate and Ball Inflation Administrator. One or another could be found wherever and whenever high stakes gambling seemed to be in bloom. Possibly all innocent but some rather remarkable overhead being sustained by 'Dunk's' office. Their compensation was not on record. I have their names and am checking any ties to Paulie the Puma."

"Fine Ursula! Thank you! I'll take it up with Agent Malamute when he calls in."

The Special Agent did just that and Octavius invited him to join us for lunch here at the hotel. The Cubs and their minders had just finished devouring everything in sight, leaving the hotel kitchen in a momentary state of shock. They waved as they scampered out, heading for Central Park. Belinda, Otto and Condo were lunching at one of New York's upscale eateries. Chita, when she heard the FBI Agent was coming, invited the Wolves to join her at a famous deli she liked very much. That left Octavius, a stealth Ursula and me to greet the FBI Dog as he entered the dining room.

It doesn't take a hotshot sleuth to recognize a nine-foot tall Kodiak accompanied by a two-foot tall Meerkat. Octavius waved him over to our table, set Ursula down on one of the empty chairs, stood and shook paws. I did the same.

"Special Agent Malamute, welcome. Assistant Director Bison told me to expect you. Glad you could join us for lunch. First, let me introduce my associate Maury Meerkat. Maury has been with me for quite some time and is a very talented investigator. Please make a selection and we can talk over our meal. Care for a drink?"

"Thanks, Doctor Bear. Just a soft drink for me."

"Good! Please call us Octavius and Maury. We've already ordered, so while you're choosing your lunch, I'll fill you in on our situation. We have been working with NYPD on the murder of Ozzie Ostrich of the Omaha Hombres. Actually, our client is Ernie Elks, manager and coach of the Gotham Giraffes. His star power forward, Joe Jeau Giraffe, was accused of killing Ozzie after they had engaged in a bar fight at the Rim Shot earlier in the evening. It turns out that Joe Jeau was taken back to his apartment after the

114

fight and passed out. The Police now believe that Joe Jeau was so drunk he couldn't have left his bed, much less catch and murder Ozzie."

"Excuse me. Let me give the waitress here my order. A coke and a cheeseburger, rare with fries on the side. Thanks! OK, so Joe Jeau is off the hook."

"He's still a person of interest but that's just a formality at this point. In a real sense, that wraps up our involvement with this case. We were hired to get him off. He really got himself freed up and that's where it could end for us."

"But it hasn't."

"Not really. I told Captain Gorilla of NYPD that we'd stay on for a few days and assist him however we can, in tracking down Ozzie's killer."

"Fine, now where do I and our Gaming Task Force fit in?"

"We have some reason to believe that Ozzie may have been killed by someone working for gamblers. He was going to file a grievance at the League for what he felt was crooked refereeing in the semi-final game that the Hombres lost to the Orlando Orbiters. That might have blown a lot of people's sweet deals. He may have been cut off at the pass before he could make the filing."

"Well, Octavius, your timing is impeccable. By the way, call me Mal. We've been gathering information on the UBA for a while now. We have reason to believe that the League has been cooperating with Paulie the Puma and other big-time gamblers all season long. I'm not sure whether 'Dunk' Duncan is in on it but there have been too many cases where scores, point spreads and even game results have been working out in the gamblers' favor.

Far too many for the law of averages to be responsible. Besides which, of course, most sports betting is still illegal and even when it's not, the IRS is not getting its share of the proceeds."

I spoke up. "We're not sure, but there are a few characters who are on the League's staff who look awfully suspicious. Try titles like: Assistant Infrastructures Manager; League Logistics Supervisor; Uniform Design Associate and Ball Inflation Administrator. A Chimp, a Lemur, a Panda, and an Afghan Hound. The Puma's an equal opportunity employer."

"You guys are good. All four of them are on our radar along with half a dozen others, including referees, timers and scorers. Where did you get your information?"

Reluctant to reveal Ursula, Octavius replied. "Just checking League employment records and past police writeups. Have there been any cases of violence associated with these guys?"

"Nothing recent or serious. Although I'm sure they know how to make threats. If you're considering one or more of them as Ozzie's possible killers, it's a bit of a long shot. Unless, of course, Ozzie got violent first. Then, things might have gotten out of hand."

I thought about that. A fight that Ozzie started. It would fit the Ostrich's character. We'd been going along believing his death was planned. It might have been spontaneous. We need to talk with Captain Gorilla. Who was Ozzie with that night?

Mal looked at both of us. "I believe we have enough evidence of game tampering to start hauling some of these worthies in for questioning and that includes 'Dunk.' That's not going to go over too well during the championship

116

finals. The media will go nuts. I'll keep you posted. Thanks for lunch and the information."

Octavius got on his phone and made an appointment with Captain Gorilla for tomorrow morning. Then he looked at Ursula and me. "Let's check out the spontaneous angle!" We agreed.

Chapter Sixteen

Mamselle Woof minds the Cubs while they play.

She corrects and protects them each day.

But addressing her, please,

Do not say Bichon Freeze.

Her name's French and it's Bichon Freezay!

If the word "spontaneous" could be applied to anyone, the Cubs would certainly qualify with a vengeance. Late in the afternoon, they had just returned from their trip to Central Park with side trips to the American Moozyum of Natural History, a dash past the "funny looking" Guggenheim and the grand Finale – the Intrepid Sea, Air and Space Moozyum.

Belinda, Octavius, Condo, Otto, Chita and I (and the ubiquitous Ursula) were relaxing in the Great Bear's suite when on cue, the doors crashed open and the whirlwinds barreled in. "Hi everyone. We had a real adventure." Once again, Mlle Woof and the Flying Tigers flopped, totally exhausted. The two Wolves strolled in just in time for the urgent report.

"We went to Central Park. It's huuuge! Then we went to the Moozyum of Natural History. They have a model of a 94-foot blue whale. Is the Prince of Whales that big, Poppa?"

"He's bigger, Arabella."

"Anyway, we saw the Titanosaur's skeleton. He's 122 feet long. I'm glad there's no dinosaurs any more. I wouldn't want to meet them."

"Birds are the descendants of the dinosaurs, Arabella."

"Birdies? Really? Oh, Gee!"

Then we went to the Hall of Gems. You'd like that, Momma. All the jewelry! Was that like the moozyum in Chicago that you protected, Poppa? ***(See Book One - The Open and Shut Case)***

"Sort of!"

"Then we went to a space show at the Hayden Platenarium."

"Planetarium!"

"That's what I said. We went out into space like we did at the NASA Space Center in Florida."

"But then, but then, we went to see the Interrupted."

"Intrepid!!"

"It's an aircraft carrier from the Great War and it has all sorts of old jet airplanes and helicopters on its deck. There's a submarine, the Growler. It's named after a fish. We went inside. I don't think I want to travel underwater in a submarine. It's scary. They also have some Space Shuttles like at Cape Candydee."

"But, but, but. You know what, Momma. They have a British Airways Concorde just like the Flying Aquabear, but it doesn't fly anymore. It once broke the record for crossing the Atlantic Ocean, but you do that all the time, don't you?"

"Sometimes, Tavi, but not always."

"Mlle Woof told us we were going to stop at Times Square and the Rocky Fellow Center tonight before we go to see The Lion King."

119

We didn't bother to correct McTavish.

Octavius said, "We have another surprise for you. Tomorrow, you'll get to play basketball with several of the Gotham Giraffes. Otto and Uncle Condo will be with you."

"Really? Oh, wow! I wish there were other kids at the Polar Paradise, so we could tell them all about what we've been doing. They'd be so jealous!"

Mlle Woof spoke up. "Arabella, McTavish. Making other people jealous is not a nice thing to do. You're very lucky that your Momma and Poppa are so rich and generous. Not every animal has your privileges. You should be good to others, not trying to make them feel ashamed."

"We're sorry, Mlle Woof. *(a paws!)* When do we eat?"

Dinner was early to allow the group to get ready for the theater. The Cubs, as usual, ran through the entire menu. We split into two parties. Mlle Woof, Octavius, Belinda and the Cubs left for Times Square and Rockefeller Center. I led the rest of the group, somewhat later after drinks, to the Minskoff Theater on W.45th Street.

The Lion King was a "roaring" success. The Cubs couldn't make up their minds whether they wanted to be Simba and Nala, the leonine hero and heroine or the comics, Warthog Pumbaa and Meerkat Timon. They immediately started calling me Timon for obvious reasons. They elected Otto to be the Warthog. They definitely didn't want to be the villain, Uncle Scar. For the rest of the evening we heard "Hakuna Matata - No Worries" over and over although McTavish would occasionally sing "I just can't wait to be King" slightly off-key.

Earlier in the evening, the Cubs had been swept away by the bright lights of Times Square and Broadway. On the way back to the hotel, they asked. "Can we have lights like those at Polar Paradise, Momma? We could advertise all sorts of stuff like the Lion and Unicorn pub and your Aquabear Review." Then when they saw Rocky Fellow Center, plans were hatched for a big skating rink in the castle courtyard and an even bigger tree for next Christmas. "We don't know how to ice skate, Poppa. Can somebody teach us?"

"When we get back to the Shetlands, I'll ask MacDougal to get you lessons. Meanwhile you have to get some sleep. You're going to play basketball tomorrow morning with some of the Gotham Giraffes or did you forget."

"No, we remember!" Arabella yawned and promptly fell asleep in Belinda's arms. McTavish lasted about 30 seconds longer.

And "The Circle of Life" made one more rotation.

Chapter Seventeen

The Giraffes play the Fabulous Four.

And a riot breaks out on the floor.

As the Cubs loudly claim

That they won the ball game,

Can we really believe the close score?

Remind me never to challenge Ursula. Remember this bit of dialogue?

"I'd love to hear Captain Gorilla's conversation with Omar."

"If you can pull that off, I don't want to know how you did it."

The AGI giggled.

Well, she did pull it off. I assume but will not ask whether she simply hacked into the NYPD recording system. Hardly legal. Our near-autonomous Artificial Intelligence system may need some additional lessons in lawfulness, rules of behavior and appropriate conduct. However, this morning, after having wrung my paws in moral dismay, I joined Octavius, the Wolves, Chita and Belinda in listening to the interview between the policeman and the basket ball star. Otto and Condo had taken the twins over to Ernie Elks' office to let them play one-on-one with several of the Gotham Giraffes. Mlle Woof tagged along. More of that later. The Flying Tigers were sleeping in. We were sitting in Octavius and Belinda's suite listening to the AGI's laptop speakers.

"Date, time, location. This is an interview between Captain Gordon Gorilla of the New York Police Criminal Investigation Division and Mr. Omar Ostrich, center for the Orlando Orbiters basketball team. Mr. Ostrich, you are

now considered a person of interest in the murder of Ozzie Ostrich of the Omaha Hombres. You are entitled to legal representation, if you so desire."

"What? You can't be serious. I don't need no damn lawyer to tell you that I had absolutely nothing to do with Ozzie's death. Where did you get such a cockamamie idea?"

"We have become aware that you are involved with the Supermodel Olivia and plan to take up residence with her after the season ends. Is that true?"

"Yeah, but what has my social life got to do with murder?"

"We are also aware that Miss Olivia had a long-standing relationship with Ozzie Ostrich."

"So, you think I got rid of Ozzie because he was shacked up with Olivia?"

"The thought did occur to us."

"Well, unthink it. I had nothing to do with that dude's death. I don't even know how, when or where it happened."

"He was beaten to death with a yet unidentified weapon. His body was found about 3 AM in an alley next to the Jefferson Circle Arena. That's the early morning after the fight between Ozzie and Joe Jeau Giraffe at the Rim Shot Sports Bar."

"So, arrest Joe Jeau!"

"We did but let him go for lack of evidence."

"So, now you're reaching for straws. Look Captain! I'm in the middle of a championship finals series. That night, when the fight broke out, Otis and I decided the best place for us to be was far away from that bar. I assume somebody broke it up, but we were long gone. We both headed back to our hotel where I went to bed to be ready for the next night's game against Oakland. We won, incidentally."

"Ozzie mentioned to a teammate that he had a very important meeting later that night."

"Well, it wasn't with me. I wouldn't have known how or where to find Ozzie even if I wanted to meet with him – which I didn't. It sounds to me like you've run out of suspects and motives and you're trying to build a case based on my affair with Olivia. It won't wash, Captain. And the next time we meet, if we do, you can damn well bet I'll have a couple of lawyers ready to sue you for false arrest. Now are we finished? I've got a date with Olivia."

"We're finished for the moment, but NYPD doesn't respond kindly to threats."

Repeat of date, time, place and participants and end of recording.

The inevitable question. "Well, what do you think?"

Octavius spoke up first. "Ursula, encrypt this recording immediately and store it someplace remote. I don't want NYPD or any law enforcement agency to think we spy on them, even if we do. I'm inclined to believe Omar. I doubt if his affair with Olivia is all that intense and if our sources are right, he has plenty of other places and potential companions at his disposal. Ozzie may have been more upset about Olivia's lack of fidelity but if he was, there is no sign that he attacked Omar. He's not showing any scars or wounds, is he? How did he behave on the court last night?"

The AGI responded. "He was exceptional. High scorer for the game which Orlando won. If he was suffering from any physical damage, it certainly wasn't showing."

Belinda looked up. "I'm no expert on testosterone. I don't even know if Ostriches have any, but I don't think a battle of the swains took place. I'm not even sure Olivia is worth fighting over. She's a knock-out. Poor choice of words, but I think her brain is even smaller than the usual Ostrich's. What do you think, Chita?"

"The Frau and I agreed that intellect was not Olivia's strong suit. Omar seems to be reasonably intelligent. I doubt if their arrangement will last that long. She's a self-centered jerk, albeit a beautiful jerk."

Frau Schuylkill nodded her head in agreement.

I butted in. "So where does that leave us? Do we fall back again on the gambling angle?

"Unless you have any more thoughts on the spontaneous scenario, we probably should. I'll contact Agent Malamute and see what is happening."

*****

Things were happening in a practice room at the Jefferson Circle Arena. True to his promise, Ernie had gathered four members of the Gotham Giraffes including Joe Jeau who was feeling relieved and grateful and only too happy to take on the Cubs. Lined up against them were the Octavian Fabulous Four – Arabella, McTavish, Otto and Condo with Mlle Woof as Cheerleader.

125

Ernie had taken the time out to act as referee, timer and scorer. Needless to say, the Cubs were bursting with nervous energy after a good night's sleep. McTavish kept shouting, "Hakuna Matata" and racing around the floor. Arabella stood under the basket, holding a ball and jumping up and down. "I can't reach it, Uncle Condo!"

The bird swooped down, grabbed her in his wings and lifted her up to the backboard while the Giraffes looked on. She almost dropped the ball but managed to get it inside the rim. Ernie shouted, "Two points for the Octavians." Cheers, barks and tail wags from the Bichon Frisé.

"Oof," said the Condor, "You're a lot heavier than the last time I lifted you." He was referring to his rescuing her from an Egyptian sand dune where she was dropped after being "cubnapped" by a very nasty vulture. *(See Book Five – The Curse of the Mummy's Case.)*

Arabella giggled, "I'm getting to be a big girl."

Meanwhile, Otto and McTavish were playing "keep away" with the Giraffes and running between their legs. Otto did his "now you see me, now you don't" routine and sprang up to the top of the backboard and dropped the ball in for a "slam dunk." This went on, back and forth, with the Giraffes "accidentally" giving away the ball to one or another of the young ursines. After about half an hour of this madcap sport, Ernie blew his whistle and declared the game over. The Octavians had won 26-20. Otto was declared MVP.

The Cubs continued to bounce the ball around as the Giraffes started off to the showers. Condo called over to Ernie and Joe Jeau. "Thanks so much. These kids will be bragging about this for weeks."

"Just as long as the media don't get a hold of it." Said Joe Jeau. "Beaten by two Bear Cubs, a Condor and an Otter. Geez!! Although I still don't know how Otto does his teleporting trick."

"Neither do we. I'm not sure he knows. All it seems to take is a shot of adrenaline and he's off. Before we go, do you have any more thoughts on Ozzie's death?"

"Ernie shook his antlers. My money is on the gambling crowd. Somebody didn't want Ozzie filing that complaint. I got a call before we came over here. The FBI and the IRS raided the League offices this morning, carting away a ton of material, computers, smart phones and the like. Nobody's been arrested...yet! 'Dunk' may be in deep doo-doo! All this while the championship is still going on. Not looking good. How much you want to bet, *(bad choice of words)* a bunch of guys on the league payroll have conveniently disappeared."

Chapter Eighteen

Malamutes look like Huskies, it's true.

But their eyes are a deep brown, not blue.

With a strange cork-screw tail

Like F-clef on the scale,

He can't bark. He just sings out "woo-woo."

Ernie was right. Back at the hotel, Octavius got a call from Special Agent Malamute, describing the raid and the immediate departure for parts unknown of a dozen League "employees." UBA Headquarters was battened down and being thoroughly searched. "Dunk" Duncan and his lawyers were vigorously protesting but thus far, to no avail. The search was specifically aimed at any connections to Paulie the Puma.

The League lawyers got far enough to permit the championship series to go ahead but some serious shifting of personnel was needed to fill some of the now absent support slots. Special scrutiny was aimed at the referees, scorers and time keepers.

The media was having a field day and one enterprising reporter from the New York Daily Scribe managed to find Octavius, playing the Joe Jeau angle. Once more, Spin Doctor Maury was called into play.

"Isn't it true that the death of Ozzie Ostrich was caused by his threat to file a complaint against the League and its referees?"

"We have no knowledge of any such connection. You might want to take that up with League management."

"Why were you called to New York in the first place?"

"Our client is Ernie Elks. When his star forward, Joe Jeau Giraffe was accused of killing Ozzie Ostrich, Ernie called on his long-time friend, Doctor Octavius Bear, a noted detective, to investigate the event. It turned out our services weren't necessary. Captain Gordan Gorilla of NYPD decided the evidence did not support guilt on the part of Joe Jeau. I suggest you talk with the Captain."

"Well, who did kill him?"

"We don't know. Again, I suggest you talk to the Captain."

"No opinions?"

"Nope!! We are taking a few days' vacation to enjoy New York and will be returning to our facilities near Cincinnati over the weekend. Thank you."

I walked back into the suite, shrugged my non-existent shoulders and said, "The power of the press has just been exerted. He was asking about the murder, not the raid. He got no news from us. Captain Gorilla may be in for another visit, however. What's Agent Malamute's take?"

Octavius responded. "He believes they have enough evidence of game tampering to file charges against the League Office and about a dozen so-called employees. None of the players or coaches seem to be directly involved. I don't know if he has anything that will stick against Paulie the Puma. He, no doubt, has an army of lawyers at the ready. The FBI and IRS will be holding a press briefing this afternoon. I suggest we stay far away from it."

The Wolves, Chita, the Flying Tigers, Belinda and I all nodded in agreement. The Octavian Fabulous Four plus One had not yet returned from the arena.

Galatea looked around and asked. "Do _we_ have any theories about who killed Ozzie?"

Octavius snorted, "I don't believe in theories unless they are supported by facts."

Colonel Where growled softly and said, "If one of the League culprits did him in, the police are going to have a tough time coming up with any proof besides motive. No witnesses, no weapon, no clues on the body. If I'm allowed to have a theory and its only based on the eternal triangle, I'd say Omar needs a bit more scrutiny. His alibi to Captain Gorilla could stand a little more support."

The Frau queried, "What was that important meeting Ozzie was going to have. If it wasn't with Omar, who was it with?"

I replied, "It may have been with one of the League officials to discuss his complaint."

Ben shook his head, "Would they meet in an alley?"

"Depends on what they were discussing and whether they wanted to keep it secret. Someone may have been trying to buy Ozzie off."

"All this is getting us nowhere." said the Great Bear. "We're heading back to Cincinnati this weekend whether this case is solved or not. Do you agree, Bel? I think the Cubs have had enough 'Noo Yuck' to last them a lifetime."

"Oh, I doubt that, Tavi but I'm sure Mlle Woof and our Flying Tigers have had more than enough of 'Raging Cubs Attack Noo Yuck.'"

Loud sigh from the two Tigers. "Where are they, I wonder?"

Question asked and promptly answered. The Fabulous Four Plus One arrived. As usual, Arabella and McTavish tumbled in the door followed by a statelier procession of Condo, Otto and Mlle Woof. "We won! We won! We beat those old Giraffes 26-20. Otto and Uncle Condo helped, and Mlle Woof was our cheerleader. We played pro Basketball at the Jeopardy Circle Arena."

"Jefferson Circle, Tavi."

"That's what I said. When's lunch?"

"Just about now and then I want the two of you to take a nap. You must be worn out. I know Ben, Gal and Mlle Woof are and I suspect Otto and Uncle Condo are too."

"We're not tired," said Arabella, stifling a yawn.

Octavius said, "We're going back to Cincinnati on Saturday."

McTavish asked, "Did you solve the case, Poppa? Who's the killer?"

"We know that Joe Jeau is not and that's what Ernie Elks asked us to find out."

"But who did it?"

"That's up to the New York Police to find out."

"I'll bet it's some nasty, tough guy."

"Maybe, it's a girl," said Arabella, yawning once again. "Let's eat!"

Chapter Nineteen

We don't know who the killer may be.

Is the culprit a he or a she?

Chita thinks she may know.

Could it really be so?

It sounds like a long shot to me.

Chita perked up her ears. 'Maybe it's a girl.' Arabella may be on to something. "Ursula, what time did we meet with Olivia the other night?"

"About eleven, Chita. The party was just winding down."

"Did she say anything about where she was the night before when Ozzie was killed?"

"No, she may have been with Omar but that's just a surmise."

"Do you think she could have been meeting with Ozzie?"

Infinitesimal pause. "She could have been."

"I think we should talk to Octavius."

The Great Bear and I were still in the suite when the others descended to the dining room in the Cubs' formidable wake.

Chita waited until the room cleared and then sidled over to the two us. "I want try an idea out on you."

"OK" said Octavius, "What's on your mind?"

"I think, and Ursula might agree with me, that we have been overlooking a possible prime suspect in Ozzie's death."

"Who?'

"Olivia the Ostrich Supermodel. Until recently, she and Ozzie had a thing going. Then, she ditched him and took up with Omar. We've been suspecting Omar as Ozzie's killer but suppose she did it. Ursula, can you play back my interview with her?"

The AGI brought up the recording. "Do you want the whole thing?"

"No, just the part about Ozzie and Omar."

"OK, here we go:

"Oh yes. I love badminton. Play it every chance I get, and I run to keep my figure in shape. But my real passion is basketball. I'm wild about it. In fact, if I didn't have a contract to be here tonight, I would be over at Jefferson Arena watching the first game of the finals. I just love the Orlando Orbiters and the Omaha Hombres. I don't care that much for Oakland."

"Anyone special on those teams?"

"Well, I did have a thing going with Ozzie from the Hombres but he's dead now."

"I heard that. They say it was murder. I'm very sorry!"

"Oh, don't be. He was beginning to be a bore. Pushy and much too demanding, if you know what I mean. We wouldn't have lasted. My current squeeze is Omar on the Orbiters. He's so much more sophisticated. He's very smooth and really talented. He's going to move in with me during the off

season. I'm going to see him after tonight's game, so I'll have to cut this short."

"Well," I said, "Aside from her loving and sentimental nature and total lack of concern about herself, what makes you suspicious? She could win a global Miss Shallowness contest."

"Couldn't she, though?"

Ursula cut in. "What you don't get from the interview is the fact that she was walking very stiffly, almost a limp. At the time, we thought it was too much alcohol but next morning, at the fashion show, she was walking the same way."

The Bear replied, "But don't all fashion models strut and walk stiffly?"

"Yes," said the Cat, "But in retrospect, this was different. I should know. I've been a runway model on and off for years. There's a sort of bounce to your strut and you hold yourself erect. She was definitely limping."

"Which leads you to conclude?"

"She kicked Ozzie to death."

"Wow," I exclaimed. "That's a stretch!"

"Not as much as you might think. An Ostrich kick can be fatal. That's their prime mode of defense and offense. Also, think about this. The Police never found a weapon, did they. They've been searching for the classical blunt instrument. That blunt instrument could be attached to the body of a female Ostrich. She's been limping because she used her legs to do Ozzie in."

Octavius whistled. *(I didn't think he could.)* I'm willing to take that theory on, even though I hate theories. Let's give a call to Captain Gorilla.

134

Ursula, will you put that conversation on a separate thumb drive. I don't want the police to know about you. Chita, it's just a recorded interview for your magazines, right?"

"Of course!"

Ursula asked me to attach a USB card to the laptop she was on and she recorded the complete dialogue. Meanwhile, Octavius called Captain Gorilla and asked for appointment later in the day. "Were on at three o'clock. Chita, will you accompany Maury and me?"

"You know how I feel about the Police…but OK."

The three of us went down to join the others at lunch. The Cubs were just finishing up and were being led off for an afternoon nap by Mlle Woof. The rest of the team were at various stages of eating. Octavius, after ordering, said to the group, "Chita has an interesting idea about Ozzie's death. I think we need to present it to NYPD but first, I want to get your reactions and input. Let's meet in the suite in half an hour."

*****

Hail, hail, the gang's all here. The Wolves, Condo and Otto took up chairs around the sitting room. Belinda was stretched out on a couch. The Flying Tigers shared a sofa. Chita and I were seated in the center of the room and Octavius, given his size and girth sat on the floor. Ursula was present in a large laptop.

The Great Bear looked around, took in a deep breath and said, "Chita has an idea I want her to share with you. Madame Catt?"

135

"In a few short sentences, I believe, and I think Ursula supports me in this, that Olivia the Supermodel kicked Ozzie to death. He may have gotten upset about her leaving him for Omar and started to push her around. She retaliated. The only weapons were her legs and sharp claws. She's been limping ever since. Ostriches can kill with a kick. I think she left him there in the alley, not knowing or caring whether he was alive or dead and has since gone on about her life as if nothing happened."

Octavius looked around. "Any responses? Thoughts? Arguments?"

At first, the group seemed dumbstruck, but it didn't last very long. The Frau shook her head and said, "Well, it would seem to fit her personality. I got the distinct impression that the only one she cared about was herself. Whether she could blithely injure someone and disappear without trying to get him help is pretty low, but I guess it's no different than a hit-and-run driver."

Otto asked, "So, you don't think she deliberately tried to kill him?"

Chita replied, "I don't know. She may just not have cared."

Condo paused for a second and then said, "That would shoot down our gamblers theory."

Belinda nodded. "But that doesn't get 'Dunk' off" the hook with the FBI and IRS and it seems very likely those guys were putting in the fix. I hope they can exonerate 'Dunk.' I like him, and he always seemed honest to me. Not super-bright if they were pulling off all that chicanery behind his back. Oh, well! What are you going to tell the Police?"

"We're going to outline our idea and suggest he bring in Olivia for an interview."

Wyatt said, "I don't suppose any of us can be there for that."

Octavius looked over at the laptop and said, "We'll see."

Ursula gently rang her chime in response. Was that a giggle?

Chapter Twenty

The Gorilla and Catherine Catt

Have a really quite startling chat.

Was the Ostrich knocked dead

From a kick to his head?

Did Olivia kill in a spat?

Octavius, Chita and I arrived at 1 Police Plaza promptly at 3PM. Captain Gorilla was waiting for us. "I thought you'd be packing up to return home."

"We're leaving on the weekend. You know Maury, but I don't think you have met Madame Catherine Catt. She is the publisher of several highly successful female's magazines in addition to a number of social media sites, other web-based offerings and TV programs. She is based in London but came to New York with us to participate in the Fashion Week shows. She is also a talented part-time detective in her own right and has been of assistance to us many times in the past. She has an idea about Ozzie's death that I'd like you listen to. But first, I suppose you know all about the raids by the FBI and IRS on the offices of the UBA."

"Yeah, I've been on the horn with Agent Malamute. That's a sorry mess but I'm not surprised. We've had several of the League's supposed executives under surveillance for a while. But now it's up to the Feds to run with this one. I'm still of the opinion that one of those thugs may have done Ozzie in to keep him from blowing the whistle on their rackets but not enough proof, yet. Now what can I do for you, Madame Catt?"

"I may be able to do something for you, Captain. I'd like to draw your attention to another potential suspect in Ozzie's demise. The Supermodel Ostrich, Olivia."

The Gorilla's face was a combination of surprise and disbelief. "I'm sorry. You think a top-rated Supermodel beat Ozzie to death?"

"Not beat, Captain. Kicked. Ostriches have been known to kill by simply using their powerful legs and clawed toes. She was in the process of ditching Ozzie for Omar of the Orlando Orbiters. We originally thought Ozzie met with Omar to have it out with him over Olivia. We know Omar vehemently denied having met Ozzie that night. So, who was Ozzie meeting? It could have been a gangster, but it could also have been Olivia. My theory is he was trying to persuade Olivia to stay with him, but she was having none of it. I have a recording of my interview with her that I'll leave with you. It's from the night after Ozzie's death. She seems totally unconcerned about his demise. I think Ozzie got a bit rough and she struck back or rather she kicked back. Then she just left him in the alley, not knowing or caring what kind of shape he was in. The reason you couldn't find a weapon was it was still attached to Olivia's body. You should know she's been limping for the past few days."

Octavius interrupted, "Now, I grant you this is only a suspicion. But you haven't gotten any closer to a solution, have you? It's your call, but I strongly suggest you have Ms. Olivia in for an interview. She may just be obtuse enough to give herself away."

The Gorilla took the USB drive with Chita's interview and placed it in his computer. He listened while the three of us waited. When it finished, he said "Well, aren't we the self-centered sweetheart. She may or may not have done him in, but she obviously didn't care that he might be dead. If she did kick him hard enough to kill him and then walk away, it may not have been deliberate, but it was certainly callous. She'll probably claim it was self-defense and it could be. We could still book her for excessive force, failure to report the incident and leaving the scene of a crime. OK, we'll have her in. Sorry, but I can't invite you to join us. I don't know if I'll need to use your interview, Madame Catt. I suppose you'd rather I didn't. We'll see how the conversation goes. As you say, Octavius, it's still just a suspicion but it appeals to me. She'll probably be heavily lawyered up when she comes. I'll let you know the outcome. Thank you all and especially you, Madame Catt. Recording finished!"

Chita turned to the two us. "I really didn't want to do that. He might discover my criminal record. I'm still wanted even if Imperius Drake and Bigg Baboon are both dead. *(See Book Five – The Curse of the Mummy's Case)* But I can't stand the idea that she'd get away with it."

The Bear smiled at her and said "Don't worry about it. We'll deal with it, if necessary. We'll get you back to London in the next few days with your publisher's identity intact" An unusual statement by Octavius who usually referred to Chita as the Female Feline Felon.

Chapter Twenty One

So, we're saying goodbye to 'Noo Yuck'

Where we forked over many a buck.

But the damage was small.

Both the Cubs had a ball,

And our client is thanking his luck.

Back at the hotel, the Cubs had overcome Morpheus and were full of energy again. Belinda had called 'Dunk' to thank him and wish him well. He was indeed tied up with the Feds but seemed to have been unaware of what was going on. Nice guy but not too bright. We checked in with Ernie and he in turn, was insistent on paying for our services. He and Octavius reached some kind of agreement, but I'm sure a minor dent was still put in the Great Bear's resources. Not for long, of course and our group, especially the Cubs, did get to "do" New York, pardon, "Noo Yuck." Joe Jeau sent Arabella and McTavish a basketball signed by all the Gotham Giraffes with an inscription that read: Octavian Fabulous Four 26 - Gotham Giraffes 20. Hakuna Matata!"

We set about getting packed up and ready for the helicopter rids back to Cincinnati. Octavius and I were then going to join Bel, the Flying Tigers, the Cubs and Mlle Woof on a supersonic run back to Polar Paradise in the Shetlands with a side trip to London to let Chita off. The Wolves, Condo and Otto were to stay on at the Bear's Lair and get updated on Howard and Marlin's progress with the "Entangled Electrons."

Ursula was monitoring the situations at the UBA and keeping track of what was happening in the ongoing saga of Olivia and the NYPD. We did get one call from Agent Malamute, telling us that they had tracked down some interesting links between Paulie the Puma and several League officials. The championship games were still going on and Orlando led Oakland two games to one.

Captain Gorilla called and said that Olivia was coming in tomorrow with her agent and lawyer. She was very upset, and her lawyer was threatening a suit for false arrest. We shall see. Meanwhile, dinner for all hands at one of "Noo Yuck's" most exclusive eateries. For once, the Cubs were on their good behavior. Hakuna Matata!

Epilogue

Back we go through the afternoon air

On our way to Octavius' Lair.

Though we had a wild chase

In this troublesome case,

Chalk another one up for the Bear.

As we descended into Harrisburg Airport to refuel, on our way back to Cincinnati, I heard Ursula's chime. Octavius and I were seated in the rear of the Ursa Minor. Belinda and the two Flying Tigers were in the cockpit and the rest of the party was spread out on the seats amidships. The Cubs of course, had window seats and were chattering about the scenery, their adventures in "Noo Yuck" and their plans for their return to Polar Paradise. Octavius had dozed off, so I answered the AGI.

"Hi Ursula. What's up?"

"I have the recording of Olivia's interview with Captain Gorilla, if Doctor Bear is interested."

"I think he will be. I'll have to wake him up."

I twitched the Great Bear's nose and he awoke with a snore-enhanced snort. "What?" he bellowed.

"Ursula has once again managed to procure a copy of Captain Gorilla's recordings. I don't want to know how. Are you curious enough to listen?"

Silence and then "Oh, what the hell. Let's hear it. Is Chita available?"

We had just landed, and the denizens of the main cabin had exited to stretch their legs. Belinda and the Tiger Twins were supervising the fueling. The Cubs were trying to get away from Mlle Woof. The Wolves, Condo, Chita and Otto were heading for the Transit Passenger lounge. I called after Chita and said, "We have something that might interest you."

The Cat turned around and entered the helicopter's rear door. Octavius looked at her and said, "Ursula captured Olivia's interview with NYPD. Highly illegal but we'll destroy it after listening. I thought you might want to hear it."

"Date, time, location. This is an interview between Captain Gordon Gorilla of the New York City Police Criminal Investigation Division and Ms. Olivia, a fashion supermodel. With her are Mr. Wellington Weasel, her lawyer and Ms. Arlene Armadillo, her agent. The subject of this inquiry is the possible involvement of Ms. Olivia in the death of Mr. Ozzie Ostrich. First off, Ms. Olivia, for the record, may we have your real name?"

"Osha Ostrich, I never use it for obvious reasons."

"Captain Gorilla!"

"Yes, Mr. Weasel."

"I have advised my client to respectfully decline to answer any questions you may have about her connection with Ozzie Ostrich's death."

"That is her right, Mr. Weasel, but of course, it will only add to the Police's suspicions about her involvement. Let me play out a scenario for you, if I may, and let us see what, if any reaction your client has to it. Ms. Olivia has been very forthcoming with the press, her colleagues and social companions about her ongoing affair with Ozzie Ostrich. Isn't that true, Ms.

Armadillo? Haven't you placed items about their romance in a variety of media columns?

"Yes, but that's just normal client hype."

"Fine. Now, she and you have also been equally forthcoming with those same audience members about her recent change of heart and attachment to Omar Ostrich of the Orlando Orbiters. In fact, our understanding is that Omar will be moving in with her at the end of the basketball season. Yes, Mr. Weasel."

"Captain, I fail to see the relevance of Ms. Olivia's love life to the subject at hand"

"We believe it is quite relevant if Ozzie Ostrich took major umbrage at what he might have believed was a betrayal. Ozzie, we are told, took offense rather easily. We interviewed Omar on suspicion that he and Ozzie had an argument over Olivia the evening Ozzie was killed. We have good reason to believe that no such argument took place. However, we do believe that Ozzie had an "important meeting" (his words) that night. We strongly suspect that meeting was with you, Ms. Olivia.

"So what? Oh, don't shush me, Wellington. Yes, I did meet him. The poor dope wanted me back. I told him it wasn't going to happen. I loved Omar and we were going to live together."

"How did he react?"

"He was angry and started to push me around."

"Olivia!!"

"Shut up, Wellington. You too, Arlene. I wasn't going to stand for that from that jerk and I kicked back."

"Hard enough to kill him? An ostrich kick can kill. Several animals have remarked that you have been limping ever since that evening."

"I fell! He was alive and unconscious when I left him."

"But you didn't see fit to report the incident or check any further on his condition"

"I didn't want get involved. I have my career to think about."

"So, you just let him die."

"Captain, I'm afraid this terminates our interview."

"Perhaps, Mr. Weasel, but based on this recorded discussion, I believe the District Attorney will want to pursue this further. There are the possibilities of charges of aggravated assault, use of excessive violence, leaving the scene and failure to report to the authorities."

"It was self-defense!! He was trying to rough me up."

"That's something for the DA and a Grand Jury to determine. Thank you for coming in. End of recording" Date, time, participants, subject.

Chita, Octavius and I all shook our heads. Octavius said "Thank you, Ursula. Let's discreetly bury that after we share it with the rest of the team. If we're ready to take off, I for one will be happy to get back home even though 'I Love New York.' " (Noo Yuck!)

The End of

Volume Nine Of the

Casebooks of Octavius Bear

The Basket Case

About the Author

Harry DeMaio is a *nom de plume* of Harry B. DeMaio, successful author of several books on Information Security and Business Networks as well as the nine-volume *Casebooks of Octavius Bear.* A retired business executive, consultant, information security specialist, former pilot and graduate school adjunct professor, he whiles away his time traveling and writing preposterous articles and stories.

He has appeared on many radio and TV shows and is an accomplished, frequent public speaker.

Former New York City natives, he and his extremely patient and helpful wife, Virginia, and their Bichon Frisé, Woof, live in Cincinnati (and several other parallel universes.) They have two sons, living in Scottsdale, Arizona and Cortlandt Manor, New York, both of whom are quite successful and quite normal, thus putting the lie to the theory that insanity is hereditary.

His e-mail is hdemaio@zoomtown.com

You can also find him on Facebook.

His website is www.octaviusbearslair.com

His books are available on Amazon, Barnes and Noble, directly from MX Publishing and at other fine bookstores.